READY TO FALL

A.K. RITCHIE

Rivers & Roads

READY
TO
fall

ISBN 978-1-7779061-2-2

ISBN 978-1-7779061-3-9 (ebook)

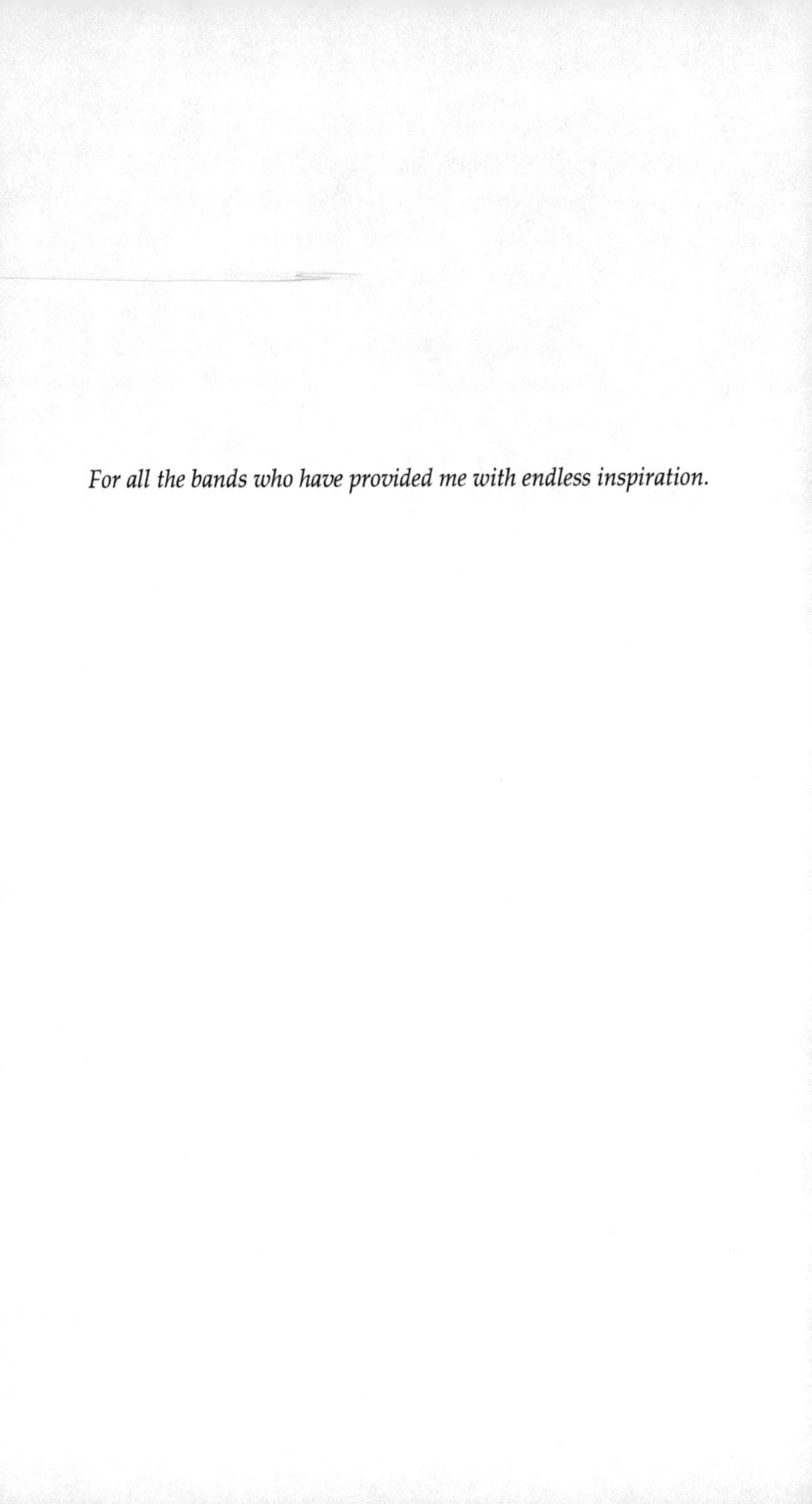

For all the bands who have provided me with endless inspiration.

1

MITCHELL

IT WAS ANOTHER NIGHT SPENT AWAKE, WAITING FOR THE REST OF
the city to join me. I sat on the windowsill, staring down the
alley toward the street. When the first signs of life appeared
below, I forced myself to return my focus back into the apartment, to the beautiful woman in my bed. Sometime that
morning, she had fallen asleep with her face between the
pillows that occupied my side of the bed. Beneath the worn
sheet, I could see the outline of her limbs spread in all directions. Her hair cascaded across the bed. She'd been lying
motionless for so long; I'd leaned down to check her
breathing before moving to the window for some fresh air.

It had been almost a month since the tour ended, almost a
month since I'd been able to sleep more than a couple hours a
night. Fall was settling into the city, but it was hard to tell
from where I sat. The change was only noticeable in warmer
attire on the people in the street and by the cold air rushing
up Bay Street. Fall usually meant the start of smaller tours for
Forever July. It meant we would be playing in clubs instead of
in an amphitheater or an exposed stage on fairgrounds. It
meant indoor toilets and bars with regular priced beer.

Fall always held good things for me and for the band. It

meant it would be the four of us out there, on the road. My mind went to the truck stop hotdogs. My legs were restless. My whole body ached for it. The magnetic calendar stuck to my fridge told me there were only twelve more days until we hit the road for two weeks. I couldn't wait to get back in the van with the boys. But I had to attend to one obligation first. There was just one thing to do before the good part.

The wedding invitation was stuck with the only actual magnet I owned. It was The Avett Brothers magnet I'd picked up on the road somewhere. I'd been to so many places, I couldn't remember what record store or even what town I bought it in.

When the invitation appeared in my mailbox, I'd slapped it on the fridge even though I RSVP'd that I wouldn't be able to attend. We had a show on that day, one I couldn't get out of. The band had only been signed with our label a year and a half before I received the invitation. I wasn't about to bail out of a label showcase.

But then we were told the venue had changed to increase capacity, and the event switched to the weekend after the wedding. The showcase fit into our already established tour, with only a few minor adjustments. I couldn't decide if the new date was a good thing or if it was a curse. Either way, I had no excuses left.

I stared at the wedding invitation.

The union of Tomasso Rizzo and Gillian Whittaker.

Tomas was exactly ten months my senior. Everyone in our hometown called us The Twins until we hit high school. The nickname always sparked tension between us. We were nothing alike and were proud of that fact. Tomas was into sports, clothes, and money. I had my music, and that became my primary focus. Tomas went from one serious relationship to the next. I had called no one my girlfriend since leaving Nine Pines.

The wedding showed how different we were, how we

were at opposite spectrums of life. He was settling down. I was moving forward.

I plucked the invitation from the fridge and held it over the trash can. I'd thought about telling them the show was still on, but I didn't want to risk someone from the wedding party calling my bluff, snitching to my brother. Those things happened in Nine Pines. I might have continued waffling about going or not, but my grandma had called the night before to tell me how much she missed me, how she couldn't wait to see me whenever I had time.

I had to make time.

One week, I told myself. I only had to get through one week and then it was back to the life I knew, the life that I built for myself.

"Do you need a date?"

I turned to face her, the woman from my bed. She ran a hand over her hair and then down over the bare, dark skin of her collarbone. The other hand gripped the sheet she had wrapped around her, barely covering her breasts. With the golden morning glow, she looked even more radiant than the night before.

Layla was the type of woman I could take to Nine Pines. From what she told me over drinks, she was doing a medical residency at St. Michael's Hospital. She grew up in a small town, so she knew what they could be like. It became apparent in no time that she had a great sense of humour. She would have been a perfect fit.

But a date to my brother's wedding meant a commitment I didn't have the capacity for. It was a commitment Layla deserved, and it was something I was incapable of. The band was my life and I had no interest in giving that up. I wouldn't let Chase, Dylan, and Mo down.

"No plus one," I lied, before tossing the invitation onto the kitchen table face down. "I'm used to going solo for these things, anyway."

She nodded as she backed toward the bed. "Well, then I better give you something to think about while you're there all alone, Mitchell Rizzo."

Being called by my first and last name wasn't something I'd gotten used to yet. After the band took off, people came to know us all by our full names. When reporters and bloggers wrote articles or talked about us in interviews, they used both our first and last names. The other boys in Forever July said it didn't bother them, but for me it was like grade school all over again. I wondered if I would ever get used to it.

"Maybe you can write a song about me." She winked and allowed the sheet to slip just a little lower on her breasts.

I remembered how effortlessly we found each other the night before. She was standing outside the women's restroom holding her friends' drinks. I'd stopped in the corridor to text a few people to see where they were at. Camila was shooting some metal band across town for her magazine, Eternal Spin. None of the boys from our band came out that night. I wanted someone to change their mind. There were people at the bar I knew, but it wasn't the same without Camila or the Forever July boys.

When I glanced up from my phone, and I found her looking at me, I stopped typing out the message to Chase. After shoving my phone into my back pocket, I smiled. She smiled back. It was just that easy.

"What's wrong?" She asked as she pulled the sheet from her body. I couldn't think of anything else while staring at all the slopes and edges of her torso. I forgot about the wedding, about my brother, about all the things I'd been avoiding in Nine Pines. I took in the softness of her hips, the curves of her breasts, the way she licked her lips while looking me in the eye.

"Nothing." I smiled. "You're perfect."

2

CHARLIE

THE ROAD CURVED TWICE, LETTING US KNOW IT WAS LESS THAN five minutes to the sign that said "Welcome to Nine Pines! Population: 19,001." The day before Hazel and I moved to Toronto, we covered the town's population with a poster board we spray painted with "18,999." According to our friends who stayed in town, it took three weeks before the make-shift sign fell apart in the rain.

"Almost home," Hazel said, at the same spot she always did. It had become part of our ritual when heading back to town for a visit and something I looked forward to every time we crossed the border into Nine Pines. As she always did, Hazel turned off the music and said, "Are you ready for a high school reunion?"

"I never am," I admitted with a chuckle. As much as I enjoyed seeing my family and friends when we came back for a visit, coming home for any event meant answering a bunch of questions people already knew the answers to. They wanted to know how school was, how I liked living in the city, if I ever planned on moving back to Nine Pines, if I was dating anyone. My parents had given them the answers to all those questions time and time again. I knew, because she sent me an email every month with details of all the things that went on while I was away. If the town newspaper had a gossip column, my mother could have submitted those emails for publication.

"Just remember, it's only until next weekend. Nine days." Hazel turned into my neighbourhood. Somehow autumn, with its warm colours, made that part of town look better than usual. Instead of looking at the cars rusting on bricks in driveways or the shingles curling on sagging rooftops, the massive old trees were the attention grabbers. There, in the oldest neighbourhood, the maples and oaks stood with thick trunks.

"Nine days. *For now.*" I shifted to look at Hazel and said, "Until Christmas comes and then I'm back for good."

Two weeks before Christmas, when I finished my very last semester, I would be returning to our hometown permanently.

Hazel kept her eyes forward. It was hard to tell if it was because I disappointed her with my decision or because she was sad to know our time together was ending. Everyone told us moving in together in Toronto would be a disaster, that friends living together was a horrible idea, but we'd become accustomed to each other's habits and knew how to avoid getting hurt by each other's flaws. It turned out to be a better fit than anyone expected, but once I finished my last class in December, it would be over. Hazel had already started looking for another roommate to take over my bedroom in January.

"That's too far away. Right now, you're in Nine Pines for nine days only. It'll fly by with all the wedding stuff and then we're back to real life in the city." Hazel eased the car along the curb in front of my childhood home. I glanced at the house, the extra cars in the driveway, the autumn wreath my mother put on the door every October.

"Then, when I get back to the city, I need to tell my boss that I won't be bar tending on weekends anymore, that they need to look for my replacement." I sighed. I'd been putting off so much and now everything was rushing at me. I needed to take the break from school to relax and forget about all the obligations I could no longer avoid. I had nine days.

"Stop. Don't think about that. Only think about this week." Hazel patted my knee with a chuckle before pushing her glasses up her nose.

"I'll try," I groaned.

"And you've got me this weekend and next week. Just five days without me," Hazel told me.

The plan had been that both of us would come back to town for the entire week together. We wanted to help out a friend who lost his father a couple months back and spend time with our families since we missed Thanksgiving the previous weekend. Thanks to reading week, I had no classes and Hazel's vacation had been approved.

Until her boss decided her job was more important than family time.

I gave her a hug before I climbed out of the car.

After grabbing my bags from the back seat, I pushed the car door shut and stood facing her. "Tell Myles I'll be by to take over a shift at the store tomorrow, so he can get a break."

"Will do."

I backed up onto the lawn, giving Hazel room to pull away from the curb. As she drove off, I turned to look at my parents' house. There used to be a comfort in the chipping paint around the windows and the overgrown garden. I used to look at the house and think about all the wonderful memories, but that feeling had been replaced with glimpses of my future. Ones I wasn't looking forward to.

The front door opened before I could crunch through the fallen leaves on the lawn. My mother stood in the doorway with a smile on her face. I smiled and remembered why I decided to come back to Nine Pines once I finished school.

My parents had done so much for me, allowed me to go to school, and found me opportunities to get out there. They deserved to be taken care of.

"We didn't think you'd be here until some time after dinner," she said, coming down the steps to meet me with her arms outstretched. I dropped my duffle bags onto the floor and allowed her to squeeze me. She smelled like mild soap and a mix of flowery scents, a perfume she put on when we had guests.

"Who's here?" I asked as I reached down to pick up my bags.

"Gillian, Amber, and Bonnie dropped by. There's been a seating chart issue and I offered to help." My mother took one of the duffle bags from my hand and said, "So, brace yourself. It's intense in there."

The instant I crossed the threshold into the house, I wished Hazel and I had driven down later like we originally planned. I set my bag onto the hardwood floor and glanced through the living room into mayhem in the small dining room. Among the hutches full of collectable tea cups and my mother's spoon collection, my cousins and aunt were in a panic.

For three people, Bonnie, Amber, and Gillian could really fill a space with chaos. Gillian was shouting into her phone at the dining room table, shouting that everything was going to go to hell. Amber was laughing at her sister's panic. Their mother Bonnie was waving her arms in front of her as she told my dad how everything about the wedding was stressing her out and she needed a deep tissue massage.

"Oh my god," Gillian screamed at the sight of me. She dropped her phone on the table, grabbed my arm and said, "Help me. Everything's a mess."

Her blonde hair bounced around with her fanatic movements. Her crystal blue eyes were wide with panic.

"What's going on?"

"Tomas' brother decided he is going to come to the wedding after saying he couldn't. So, we had to bump a groomsman, who then decided he and his girlfriend weren't going to come to the wedding at all. Now we have two empty chairs with no one to fill them, and on top of that Uncle Deon and Rima split. They both still want to come to the wedding, but to sit at different tables." Gillian dragged me into our tiny, already crowded dining room to look at the Bristol board seating chart. "See? It's a mess."

I glanced down, hoping to see a quick solution so the conversation could stop, but I noticed my name on a little sticky note on one side of the table, three seats down from the bride. Three seats down from the groom, on the opposite side of the table was a person I was not expecting.

"Um..." I glanced up at Gillian.

Her pale face was flushed, and she kept tugging on a strand of her hair. Her eyes widened. "Don't tell me you brought a date. Actually, can you bring two dates and we can sit one with Rima and one with Deon?"

"I thought I was walking down the aisle with Lucas," I said. My brother and I planned a full, goofy dance to enter the reception with. If we had to be paired together, we would make a scene. As much as I wouldn't miss dancing and walking the aisle with my brother, the name on the piece of paper made my entire body tense.

Gillian rolled her eyes and said, "You're paired up with Mitchell."

"I thought he was supposed to be on tour or something." I tried to act cool, but the ridiculousness of the situation wasn't lost on me. Mitchell Rizzo had been my brother's friend. Mitchell Rizzo had barely acknowledged my existence when we were kids. Mitchell Rizzo had been my high school crush.

"He's back." Gillian fanned at herself with a piece of paper from the table. "He's just going to get in the way. Like, why is he even here? Mitchell and Tomas don't even get along. This is going to be a disaster."

I stared at the seating chart on the table in front of me and wondered if her statement was foreshadowing.

3

____

MITCHELL

Taking the wrong turn into my hometown was a reminder of how little I visited. As much as I wanted to blame it on distraction, the confusion came from the addition of a new stop sign and the fact I avoided Nine Pines as much as possible.

It hasn't been long enough, I thought to myself as I drove between the rows of now-empty cottages. The place has become so expensive because of people moving to Nine Pines from cities all over the province, it forced the locals to move further away from the lake's waterfront. I navigated the car away from the beaches and back into the heart of town, away from the area people knew from countless social media posts or articles about Ontario's best beaches.

According to the address he'd given me, Tomas had rented a house near the northernmost part of town. It turned out to be a tiny house on a large grass lot. There was a dog barking in the window that made me wonder if I'd pulled into the wrong driveway. While our conversations remained limited, I assumed he would have mentioned if he bought a dog. It was the kind of mundane thing we discussed when we did talk.

The black Lab kept barking as I parked and made my way to the front stoop. I couldn't help wondering if they would hear my knock over the dog's noise. Someone should have already come to the door, I realized while knocking anyway.

As I waited, I glanced at the houses all around me. The only thing my brother and I had in common was the desire not to live and die in some suburban neighbourhood in Nine Pines. I knew it was a rental house, but I wondered why he hadn't tried looking for an apartment downtown until he could get out of here. Tomas always talked about living on the coast. He wanted to be in B.C. so he could hike, climb, surf, and scuba dive.

When the dog finally gave up, I did too. No one answered the door. I took the phone from my pocket and shot off a quick message, asking Tomas where he was. Despite my detour, I was right on time.

His response came only seconds later.

shit forgot ill be a bit

I shook my head in disappointment as I typed out a response.

i'll be at gma's.

It shouldn't have surprised me they forgot I would be there. I only got the invitation to the bachelor party a week before it happened, even though they picked a bar only a fifteen-minute streetcar ride from my place in Toronto. I tried not to think about it, but it replayed in my mind over and over as I drove across town to my grandma's house.

When I talked about going home to visit family, it was her little bungalow I spoke about. That tiny, two-bedroom house is where I was most comfortable. It would have been where I stayed for the week were it not for my aunt and uncle flying in from St. John's for the wedding and taking the guest room.

Before I put the car in park, my grandmother appeared on her front porch in a butter yellow sweater and the largest grin on her slender face. As I climbed out of the driver's side, she waved and said, "I didn't expect to see you yet."

"I went to Tomas' house, but I guess he's busy." I leaned forward and planted a small kiss on her cheek. Giving her bony shoulder a squeeze, I said, "But that gives me extra time to come hang out with you."

"Have you called your mom or dad yet?" She asked as I opened the door for her. She used my hand to support herself as she stepped back inside the house.

"Yup. Dad's busy today. Mom said the key is in its usual place. I guess I'll see them both eventually."

We both knew it was a stretch.

I cleared my throat before I went on. "I changed my mind. I'm going to stay at Mom's so I don't get in Tomas' way."

Instead of asking me anything else about them, she put a hand on my wrist. Her dark eyes bore into mine, as if she was trying to reassure me without words. She squeezed my arm and said, "I'm glad you're back."

I could do without Nine Pines. I could also do without seeing my parents. The people left in town didn't matter much to me, but I was glad to have the time with my grandmother.

THE TELEVISION WAS PLAYING JEOPARDY WHEN MY GRANDMA FELL asleep. I got up from the couch and cleaned up the dishes from the super basic dinner I had thrown together. I cleaned them and put them away. One less thing for her to worry about when she woke up.

The house needed some love. It didn't look like the kitchen floor had been swept in a while, so I did a few chores around the place before heading out to the sunroom outback. The place was full of plants. Every inch of window space was filled with them. In the far corner was the Monstera Deliciosa

I'd taken a clipping from when I first moved to Toronto. I stroked one of its massive leaves before ducking beneath them to check the soil. It was perfect. Like the rest of the house, I feared the plants were neglected, but my grandmother loved that room and had devoted her life to growing her collection.

She had some rare plants and she allowed me to take cuttings to sell online when things were getting expensive for me in the city. The last time I bought her a bus ticket into the city for a weekend, she'd been impressed by what I'd managed to grow in my own place. It wasn't even close to what she'd created in her sunroom, but I loved it.

I took the phone out of my pocket and texted my best friend, Chase, reminding him that I'd left the watering and care schedule on my kitchen table and to message me with questions. I didn't want to go home to yellow leaves or aphids on everything, but texting him wasn't necessary. Chase, the lead singer of our band Forever July, was easily the most responsible person I knew. The calendar on his phone would already have all the dates and times scheduled for watering. He would even have little notes about which to water, instead of worrying about the piece of paper I left with instructions. There was no reason to worry about him. The message was more for me. It was a reassurance somehow.

In the middle of typing out the text, an incoming call appeared on my screen from Tomas. I swiped to answer it.

"Hey," I said into the phone.

"Little brother." There was a lot of noise in the background, a lot of voices. By the sound of the dog barking in the background, I assumed he was finally home and he brought a bunch of people with him.

"Where are you?" I asked, hoping he would tell me the truth.

"Can you stay at Mom's tonight?"

"Yeah. I was planning on it." I hoped he would under-stand I'd made the plan because he'd forgotten my arrival.

"Gillian and I want some alone time tonight."

They were about to spend the rest of their life together and they needed to have 'alone time' on the first day I was supposed to stay with them? I tightened my grip on my phone.

"Mom's not there. She's staying with Todd. She said you can have the house for the week as long as you don't fuck it up."

It sounded like Tomas and our mother talked longer than my mom and I had.

"Yeah, that's fine."

"And can you go to Lucas' parents house when you're leaving Grandma's? Gillian forgot her wallet there. Can you bring it to the bar when you come tonight?"

"Yeah, I guess."

"You're the best. See you tonight."

He didn't wait for a response before disconnecting the call. I shoved it back into my pocket. After a moment to calm down, I lumbered back into the living room where I found my grandma collecting her teacup from the table beside her.

"Hey Grams, I have to go." I took the mug from her and said, "I'll be back tomorrow."

After making sure she had everything she needed and planting a kiss on her cheek, I grabbed my coat and my keys. She stood in the front window as I backed my car down the driveway. By the time I stopped, about five houses down, she'd already closed over the curtains.

I left the car running as I jogged up to the front of Lucas Whittaker's old house. By the time Lucas and I had estab-lished a solid friendship through bonding over our general dislike of everything, we were both in high school. I'd only been inside the Whittaker house a handful of times. Lucas didn't like how his parents were always on his case about who he was hanging out with and where he was going at night. Since I'd never been good with adults, we always opted to hang out anywhere but at his house.

As I knocked on the door, I wondered if they would even remember me.

But I didn't have to worry, because neither of his parents appeared. A doe-eyed, curvaceous woman answered the door. She stared at me but said nothing. It took me several seconds to realize why she looked so familiar.

"Little Charlotte Whittaker?" I asked, eyebrows arched.

"Yes." She wrinkled her nose for a second. "But it's Charlie. Not Charlotte."

From what I could remember, she'd always been shy. I didn't think she'd ever said that many words to me before.

While Lucas and I were in high school, Charlie was still in middle school. I hadn't even known Lucas had a sister until she walked into the living room one day after school. She'd stared at me while munching on a carrot. Lucas asked if she wanted to play Mario Kart with us, but she'd just turned around and walked away.

The few times I stopped by the Whittaker house after that, she'd always been hiding somewhere else, only appearing for food or drinks. Unlike some of my other friends' siblings, she never hung around, never tried to tag along. She didn't seem interested at all in what we were doing.

That round face staring up at me now was nothing like the awkward kid I remembered. She'd turned into a beautiful woman.

I smiled. "Charlie. It's been a long time."

"Yup."

"You're still not a big talker, huh?"

She shrugged.

"I'm here to pick up Gillian's wallet. She left it here."

"Oh." She nodded and pushed auburn waves from her face. She left the door open while she walked down the hallway into the kitchen at the other end of the house. As she moved, I couldn't help but notice she wasn't a skinny kid who was all limbs anymore. Even beneath the baggy sweater, I could tell she had a figure that rivaled Marilyn Monroe's. She wasn't nearly as tiny, but those curves...

"Are you coming out to the Tavern tonight with the rest of the wedding party?" I asked her as she walked back toward me.

She stretched out her hand, offering the wallet to me. "Doubt it. I wasn't really planning on it."

There were beautiful women in town, but none would pique my interest the way she had by simply opening the door.

"Come on. I heard you and I are pairing up for the wedding. We're going to be walking down the aisle together, so it would only be right if we both show up."

Her cheeks flushed red.

"I just mean, it would be cool if the whole wedding party was there. A 'get to know each other' thing before the big day," I said, hoping to make her less uncomfortable.

"We'll see." She took a step back from me. The space was deliberate. She put her hand on the door, letting me know the conversation was over. "Maybe I'll see you there."

I took a step away, giving her the space she wanted. "If not, have a good night and I guess I'll be seeing you around town."

She didn't say anything else, but shut the door before I'd even turned away.

4

CHARLIE

"JUST COME OUT," I WHINED INTO THE PHONE. "I DON'T WANT to go to The Tavern alone."

The sound of The Goonies playing in the background told me she wouldn't be leaving the house that night, but I had to try. When Hazel decided on a retro movie marathon, it meant she was in sweatpants, wearing no bra, and in bed for the night. She confirmed my suspicion with a solid, "Nope. Too bad."

"You're mean," I groaned, throwing myself back onto my childhood bed. I'd been trying to wear her down for almost ten minutes, and her responses were only becoming more solidified. We'd reached the point where I knew there was no winning.

In true Hazel fashion, she chuckled into my ear. She didn't see the point in continuing the argument.

"Fine. I guess I'll just go and embarrass myself in front of my high school crush all by myself," I told her. It was a last ditch effort, but I couldn't give up without at least trying it. I wouldn't do anything to humiliate myself in front of Mitchell, but I was banking on Hazel feeling a shred of remorse for me.

Hazel knew all about my crush on Mitchell. It started in

middle school, when he and my brother began spending time together. Before that, he was just another guy in our very small town. Mitchell was mysterious in his own way. He didn't seem interested in popularity and in high school he walked the hallways with the aloofness of someone much older than he was. He appeared unfazed by the drama of teenage life. If he was hanging out with Lucas at our house, he'd always disappear right before my parents walked through the door. I always wondered why. He made me curious.

Hazel let out a loud laugh and said, "I have it on good authority that Mitchell is really into hooking up with random people, so you should take a shot at it."

"Yeah. I can't imagine that going well." I stared at the popcorn ceiling, trying to think about all the ways it could blow up in my face if I followed her suggestion. One, my brother's head would explode if he saw one of his friends with me. Two, everyone in town would know about the situation before we'd even reached his house. A one night thing would be talked about for years to come. Three, every time Mitchell and I were both in Nine Pines, people would orchestrate ways to push us together. It happened with Hazel and her ex, James, so often that Hazel made a point of hiding out when she came back to town.

Hazel snorted a laugh into the phone. "Why not? You've had your fair share of random hook-ups. And you've been with hotter men."

"I don't know about hotter. Are you sure about that?"

"Definitely."

"I highly doubt that, Hazel." I tried to think about it, but Mitchell's arm muscles bulging through the fabric of his sweater consumed my thoughts. "And, I think maybe I have him on a pedestal. He's this amazing musician. He's successful. He's got this sexy, I-don't-care-about-anything-or-anyone vibe. I'll get seduced by it."

"You're already seduced by it."

We laughed at her honesty.

"That's why I need you there."

"My dad and I have four old movies to watch tonight, so you're on your own."

"Fine." I sighed. "But if I end up emotionally crushed by him after being physically crushed by him, you're going to have to deal with my sobbing and binge eating for at least a week."

Hazel sucked in a deep breath. "Don't take this the wrong way, but I would rather deal with you sobbing over Ben and Jerry's for days than spend even an hour at The Tavern on a Friday night."

I wanted to be frustrated with her for not coming, but I couldn't be. Hazel had been working non-stop, even most weekends, at the new job her father landed her. She came home exhausted every night and woke up tired too. I knew how much she needed the weekend to relax with her family. And even though she wasn't working for the law office, she was helping out at Myles' store. Making her feel bad about wanting to take her only free weekend to herself was a terrible thing to do on my part.

"That's fair." I pushed myself up from my bed. "I guess I should get ready. Lucas is picking me up any minute now."

"Think about what I said," Hazel told me in a motherly voice.

I went to my old desk, where I'd dumped the make-up I brought along. "Think about what?"

"Hooking up with Mitchell."

I let out a long 'hmmm' into the phone and I sat down in my desk chair.

"You're moving back to Nine Pines in December. You have a lifetime of focusing on other people and taking life too seriously, right? At least spend the next couple of months having fun and doing things for you."

I sat there with the phone pressed against my ear, thinking about her statement. I had no idea if Mitchell would even want to hook up with me, if he was at all attracted to me, but the idea was as exciting as it was terrifying.

Hazel was right. I deserved to have a little fun before I started focusing on nothing other than paying off all the student loans and making sure my parents still had a roof over their heads.

"I'll think about it."

"You have plenty of time for settling down in the future and that's coming up sooner than you think. Right now, just allow yourself to have a good time. Get wild. Make memories and all that. Nothing serious. Just some fun."

Hazel always knew how to make me emotional.

"I don't deserve you."

"Obviously not," Hazel said, her tone full of sarcasm. "Wear that black bodysuit that shows off your side boob. Pair it with some black jeans and a lot of eyeliner."

"Um, that's not suitable for The Tavern. I can't go out in Nine Pines showing off my boobs."

"Then why did you pack it if you didn't want to wear it? Put a flannel shirt over it, just don't button it up so that you can entice Mitchell Rizzo with sneak peaks of side boob when no one else is looking."

"Oh god. This is sounding a little complicated." I laughed.

"You're considering it, right?"

I sighed and Hazel let out a hoot of amusement.

"Have fun," she told me. "Text me when you're home and let me know if you're safe in your bed. *Or* Mitchell's."

"Goodbye," I bellowed into the phone. Hazel chuckled to herself and ended the call without a goodbye. I tossed my phone onto the desk and grabbed my old make-up mirror from where I left it in the closet the last time I was in town. With my foundation brush in hand, I stared at my reflection, contemplating. If I hooked up with Mitchell tonight, it would be awkward at the wedding. But Hazel was right; I deserved a little fun. I'd dress cute and flirt a little. I'd laugh at all Mitchell's jokes, re-apply my lip gloss a hundred times, and compliment his band. Whatever happened after that...

"Charlie," Lucas shouted up the stairs. "We're heading out in twenty minutes."

I reached down into my duffle bag at my feet and pulled out the bodysuit. Hazel was right. I deserved a little fun.

FRIDAY NIGHTS AT THE TAVERN ALWAYS BROUGHT OUT A WEIRD combination of people. The farmers were in after a long week, the regulars still occupied the stools at the bar they had silent dibs on, and families hung around at the far tables until the bartenders asked them to leave at ten-thirty. Then there was the younger crowd of townies, where I would fit in that night. They were loud and crowded around the far side of the bar, taking over several tables as well. Unlike high school, no one split off into groups. If you were under thirty, you hung out together at The Tavern.

There was nothing modern about The Tavern. Even though smoking indoors was banned before I was born, I could swear the smell of cigarettes still hung in the air. It likely clung to the sections of maroon and forest green carpets in the dining area. There were pictures of baseball and hockey players in frames on the wall, most of which were yellowing from age. There was a whole feature wall dedicated to NASCAR. Some images in the feature wall looked to have been torn from old calendars.

Tonight, Gillian and Tomas were wearing Bride and Groom trucker hats, leftovers from the bachelor and bachelorette parties they had a few weeks earlier. Lucas pushed his way into the middle of the crowd and flung his arms around the soon-to-be bride and groom, giving them exaggerated kisses on the cheek. I hung back, scanning the crowd until I saw who I was looking for.

Mitchell was already there with a beer in one hand and his arm around the shoulders of a beautiful woman who was dressed in such high-end clothes no one would mistake her for a local.

When Gillian split from the crowd, I touched her arm and asked, "Who is that?"

"Nina, she's my best friend from college," Gillian said as she linked her arm through mine. "And she's one of my bridesmaids! It goes Amber, Nina, and then you in the wedding processional. Have you not met her?"

Before I could answer, she dragged me toward Mitchell and Nina. I tried to dig my heels into the sticky floors, but Gillian was on a mission. It looked like my plan to play it cool was about to be squashed. Gillian yelled to Nina as we approached and said, "I want you to meet my cousin. She's the one that fixed the whole seating chart issue this afternoon."

"Hi," I said, making a point of not looking at Mitchell right away. I shook Nina's hand before turning to look at him, giving a casual nod. Or what I hoped was a casual nod.

Mitchell was wearing a black dress shirt under a black blazer. I'd never seen him dressed up before. From the few pictures I'd seen online of him with his band, he didn't often dress in anything other than hoodies, t-shirts, and jeans. I glanced down to see he was at least still in jeans and a pair of Vans.

"Thank you for doing that. Like, your family has so much drama, I just took one look at it and thought, someone else should really handle this." Nina gave me a wide grin.

"Did I say that Nina and I were roommates while I was at Camosun College? I wanted to make Nina my maid of honour, but I knew Amber would make a scene if she didn't get that spot," Gillian said.

I knew all too well that Gillian's sister wouldn't have taken that news well. I also knew better than to agree with Gillian in case word got back to her sister about it. Without meaning to, I glanced back over at Amber.

Gillian turned to Mitchell and gestured to Nina. "And how do you two know each other?"

Mitchell's arm slipped off Nina's shoulder. "We were both ordering Kronenbourg."

"Speaking of beer, I need a drink," I said, turning toward the counter. I glanced down to see the lineup of people all waiting to be served. The bartender, Ralph, didn't even have time to look in our direction.

"Don't hold your breath," Gillian said with a groan. "Stacey called in sick."

Mitchell leaned over the bar and said, "Hey Ralph, can I get back there?"

"You got Smart Serve?" Ralph hollered back.

"Nope."

"Then you belong on that side of the bar." Ralph laughed.

If I wanted a drink, I could get behind the bar and help out. As Mitchell was already busy with Nina, I couldn't see any reason not to get back there. It would make my night easier if I was preoccupied making drinks until Lucas was ready to go home. Then I could say that I showed up and put in my time at the event. Plus, if I could work for tips, that would be money I could put toward getting tickets for one of my favourite bands, The Head and the Heart.

"I have my Smart Serve," I shouted down the bar. Ralph stopped serving, looked me over, and said, "I'll pay you seventy-five dollars and you get tipped out."

Without hesitation, I slipped between Gillian's clustered wedding party and ducked under the counter. I grabbed a bar rag from the bucket and checked the place out. Everything was sticky. Ralph called me over to show me how to use the register, which turned out to be as standard as they came.

"You think you got it?" Ralph asked while popping off the lid of three beers, one after another. His face said he was unsure, but his options were limited.

I nodded and headed back to the far side of the counter.

Gillian waved at me and shouted over the country music, "Tequila sunrise!"

Before I knew it, everyone from the wedding party turned and started trying to get my attention for drinks. It only took me a few orders before I got into the swing of it.

There was something about being behind the bar that I always loved. Because I had desperately needed money, I started by bussing at a bar near my apartment called The Dive. Not only did they pay for me to get my certification when they needed a new bartender, it turned into something I loved, something I would miss when I finished school.

Mitchell squeezed between two truckers and asked, "You know how to make a Manhattan?"

"I do. But only if you don't mind Manhattans in plastic cups," I said, grabbing a cup from the stack on the counter. The way he tilted his head to the side, showing off the hint of a tattoo beneath his shirt, caused tingles to shoot out all over my body from my chest.

5

MITCHELL

"I'LL LIKE IT ANYWAY YOU GIVE IT TO ME," I TOLD CHARLIE. I expected her to blush or turn away like she had only hours earlier. Instead, she looked me right in the eye and laughed. Leaning forward, she collected my money from the counter without breaking eye contact.

The shy version of Charlotte Whittaker disappeared when she was pouring drinks and popping the tops off bottles. While Nina and Gillian talked to each other, I kept my elbows on the bar, watching Charlie work. Though I knew very little about Lucas' sister, the woman in front of me wasn't a version of her I'd ever witnessed before. She chatted with everyone, laughing at their jokes and nodding when they said something serious.

She was working for tips; I knew that, but it took a confidence I didn't realize she had. She wasn't quiet Charlotte Whittaker.

I turned my back to her and the bar to look at Nina and Gillian. Nina gave me a smile and while I returned it, my heart wasn't in it anymore. It didn't seem fair to divide my attention between her and Charlie. And Charlie definitely had the bulk of it.

"She wasn't being weird, was she?" Lucas asked as he broke through the crowd.

"Who?"

"Charlie."

I held still so as not to give anything away.

"My sister. Charlotte." He raised his eyebrows, concerned that I didn't know. I'd played the part well.

"Oh." I chuckled. "No, not at all."

"I think she had a crush on you when she was like fourteen or something," Lucas laughed.

"How old is she now?" As soon as the words were out there, I wanted to take them back. There were very few people in Nine Pines who messaged me every time I returned, and Lucas was the only one who didn't care about the band, about how much money I was making, if I was sleeping with a lot of girls, or if I was meeting famous people. He wanted to hang out when I was back in town like in the old days. I didn't want to mess up that relationship.

"She turned twenty-three this past August." Lucas told me.

The three-year difference was nothing, but the fact that she was Lucas' sister was something. Not only would Lucas be pissed, but there was a tie to Charlie that I wouldn't be able to avoid. We would run into each other again; I was certain of it. Especially now that Tomas was marrying Gillian. Gillian and Charlie were cousins.

As tempting as it was, I didn't know Charlie enough to know how cool she would be with something casual. If I asked, especially if she wasn't interested, that would get back to Lucas.

I took a risk and glanced at her again. At some point, while I was distracted with Lucas, she'd pulled her hair up into a messy ponytail. My eyes trailed down her neck to where the flannel shirt was sliding off her porcelain shoulder.

Lucas draped himself over the bar and yelled out to his

sister. She flipped him the middle finger as she reached for a bottle of vodka on the back shelf. A bunch of people hollered in rowdy amusement and one guy even threw a twenty on the bar, declaring it her tip.

Nina placed perfectly manicured fingers on my bicep and asked, "Did you want to get a table?" She nodded her head toward the empty one at the far side of the place. There would be no one around to interrupt us. It was intimate. Any other night, I would have been over there with Nina without a second thought, but Charlie came back over to our side of the counter to give Lucas a beer.

"My brother wouldn't like it too much if I didn't join in on the festivities," I said. Anyone else from Nine Pines would know how much of a lie that was, but it was an excellent answer for the situation, one that left no one's feelings hurt.

Nina pouted her lips for less than a second before one shoulder popped up into a shrug. As she walked away, she sashayed her hips a reminder of what I was letting slip through my fingers. I had to admit, following her to a dark corner of The Tavern was tempting.

"You wanna get high?" Lucas asked when Nina had cleared enough distance between us. He pulled a joint from the breast pocket of his button-up shirt and held it up like a trophy.

"Definitely," I said before tipping the rest of my Manhattan into my mouth. When I placed the cup on the counter, Charlie snatched it up and tossed it into a bin behind her. I wanted to say something to her, but I kept my mouth shut.

"Another?" She asked.

"He's coming out with me," Lucas said. He nodded toward the exit. I raised one shoulder in a silent apology and followed Lucas out into the cool October air.

There were a few older men out in front of the Tavern, standing in the parking lot, but they paid no attention to the two of us. Lucas put the joint between his lips and lit it. Even without smoke, I could see my breath in the air in front of me. I rubbed my arms and asked, "How you been, man?"

"Been fucking better," Lucas said as he exhaled smoke between us. He took another puff before passing the joint to me. "My hours got cut at the garage, but things will pick up."

The smoke burned on the way down, but I held it in.

"I hope they do," I said before coughing the smoke out of my lungs.

"Lucas," a woman's voice came from between a set of cars. I vaguely remembered her from high school, but her name eluded me. She walked over and said to Lucas, "Introduce me to your friend."

"Kara, this is Mitchell. Mitchell, Kara."

I remembered Kara. I'd bought weed from her a handful of times when my regular guy wasn't available. Rumour around town was that her father gave her the weed to sell on his behalf. There were also rumours that he kept a property out on the edge of town, which left many people with a lot of suspicions of what went on out there. I steered clear of that situation as often as possible. So often people romanticize small towns like Nine Pines. They had no idea the kinds of things that went on when the tourists were gone for the season. It looked like a storybook from the outside, but from the inside, the dark corners were noticeable.

"Mitchell Rizzo. Heard you're famous now," Kara said in a dreamy voice. She leaned against Lucas, resting her head on his shoulder. Her eyes were bloodshot and her mouth twitched several times before she forced a smile.

"I wouldn't say famous, but we're doing good."

"You're famous. I saw your band's Instagram. The girls basically just throw themselves at you, huh?" Kara closed her eyes for a second, and I wondered if she ever planned on opening them again. When I didn't answer, she turned to Lucas. "Rails?"

"I'm in," Lucas said without hesitation. He looked at me. "Wanna do some lines?"

"I'm good," I told him. I attempted to hand back his joint, but he waved it away. "It's all yours."

On the road, I might have done a line or two of cocaine in some seedy bathroom like The Tavern. The thought of doing any more than drinking and smoking weed in my hometown made me uncomfortable. It was impossible to tell who was watching, who knew your parents, or worse – your grandmother.

"Remind me to get your autograph later," Kara said as she looped her arm through Lucas'. They headed into the bar before I could think of a nice way to say no to that plan.

I thought about standing out there, finishing the joint on my own, but the old guys next to the Ford F-250 were staring at me. I wondered if they were friends of my dad's, or maybe my mom's. Would they tell my parents they saw me smoking outside? I assumed they made assumptions about my life-style. My family had hinted that they knew about my partying when I was in Toronto or on the road. There were plenty of pictures on my open social media as evidence, but only my brother followed my accounts.

I put out the joint on the bottom of my shoe and headed back into the warmth. The first thing I saw when I crossed the threshold was Charlie Whittaker making a drink with one hand while doing a shot with Gillian. As she raised her arm and tilted her head back, her shirt fell away, exposing the white skin of her rib cage and a tattoo there I couldn't make out from the distance.

As much as I wanted to get a better look, I turned away.

I sucked in a deep breath and reminded myself, *she's Lucas' sister.*

6

———————

CHARLIE

Despite being behind the bar all night, I had a good time. It didn't feel like work because Ralph handed me shots to do with him during the night. I was warm from the drinks by the time things slowed down at midnight. By two o'clock, when Ralph told everyone to go home, I was drunk and had spent the night socializing with everyone from the wedding party.

Lucas had been missing for most of the night, but when things cleared out, he was easy to spot. He was sitting at a table at the back of the place, looking really out of it. Mitchell sat in front of him, texting and eating the last of the fries he'd ordered earlier. Mitchell looked up at me and said, "Wanted to make sure you two got home safely."

I took the cash Ralph gave me for my work and grabbed the jar I'd been using to collect my tips. I ducked under the counter and as I stood, said, "That's nice of you. Probably for the best, because I don't think I can carry him back by myself."

An hour or two earlier and I might have been excited that Mitchell was alone and looking pretty sober. If I was being honest, a fraction of me still was. But I realized how questionable of an idea it would be to sleep with him. They had paired us up in the wedding, and we would have wedding things to do together during the week. If it ended up being awkward, there would be no escaping that. Plus, the whole town would pick up on it in an instant. And if I had no plans of returning to Nine Pines after school, that might not have mattered to me. In a couple of months, I would be back and I wouldn't have the anonymity of the city to hide any embarrassing hook-up stories.

After goodbyes to Ralph, we headed out of the bar into the crisp night air. In the summer, there would have been options to take a cab, but those options dwindled to one after the tourists went home. I might have been able to call someone to come get us, but it would take less time to make the walk back.

"You know, I've been to the bar your brother said you work at," Mitchell told me as we cut across the town square. All the businesses were dark, but the square itself was still bright with street lights made to resemble old, kerosene street lamps. I glanced up at Mitchell and noticed he was watching me while waiting for an answer.

Lucas mumbled that he didn't need help walking, but Mitchell kept his arms wrapped around my brother's back. Lucas' feet scuffed along as we moved along.

"I'm surprised I didn't notice you," Mitchell went on. "When I went to the bar."

I thought about all the flirty responses I might have given him even a couple of hours ago, but I'd come to terms with it being a terrible idea. I'd let my teenage memories get in the way. Instead, I just shrugged. "I work at the back bar, off the side of the dance floor."

"Maybe the next time I'll come to the back bar and say hello."

I looked up at him, and he grinned at me.

It was right there, the chance to say something suggestive, to let him know I was interested. That moment could be the tipping point between sleeping with Mitchell and not sleeping with Mitchell.

"How's your band?" I asked, changing the subject.

Even though I averted my eyes on the road ahead, I could feel his on me. I tried not to read into it. I'd witnessed first-hand how personable he was. He made eye contact with everyone he spoke with all night. He could make people smile with just a word or two. I reminded myself it was his job to be personable. He had literal fans. It wasn't out of the realm of possibility to think some kids somewhere had posters of him on their walls.

"The band is good. We just got back from a tour a couple weeks ago. Been trying to settle into being home again." Then, without prompting, he asked, "I heard you're moving back here after school. Why?"

"What? Snitches," I said with a laugh. "I am, but who told you?"

Mitchell let out an amused chuckle that seemed to come from deep in his chest. "Basically everyone."

Lucas snapped his head up from Mitchell's shoulder and said, "I snitched."

We took a path that ran between two houses and came out into my neighbourhood. It was so dark I didn't think Mitchell would catch me looking at him, taking in his tall frame, the slight scruff on his jaw, how broad his shoulders were. I might not have been able to see the colour of his pupils in that light, but I definitely knew when he caught me staring. I glanced away, trying to make it seem as casual as possible.

"So, you never said why you're moving back." He adjusted Lucas' weight, and we kept going.

I took a few seconds to think of a way to say it without hurting Lucas' feelings. While it was the truth, it wouldn't ease the awkwardness. I didn't know if he would remember the next morning, but I didn't want to take a chance.

"It's not that I really want to, but my family needs help. They've put a lot of money into me going to school and I think it's only right that when I can make money, I help them out the way they helped me."

"Oh, cool," Mitchell said, without sounding at all like it was cool. "What are you in school for?"

"I'm finishing my MBA."

"That's big."

I shrugged and then laughed. "It's something."

"So, you're telling me you don't have some intense love of business?" He asked. Even in the lack of light, I could see him smile.

"Nope. Not even a little bit. Just thought I would lean into capitalism. Can't beat 'em, join 'em, right?" I hoped the sarcasm was obvious. Just to make sure, I clarified, "I didn't know what to do, so I decided I would take business in case I ever wanted to open a store or bar or something on my own."

We turned onto my street.

"If you could do anything, what would you do?" He asked.

At the beginning of my university career, it was all I thought about. There were so many plans, so many options, but as I learned more about business and more about myself, the financial situation my parents were in became clear. I knew we didn't have money growing up, but the magnitude of it was lost on me until I was in the city. Despite their struggle, my parents always tried to give me everything they could.

"Can you answer first while I think about it?" I asked him with a light chuckle.

"I'm doing what I always wanted to do," Mitchell said. "I've got the band. We make enough money to live off of, mostly. So, I guess what's next is...I don't want to worry about money anymore. But career wise, I'm doing what I've always wanted. Maybe just not at the level I wanted."

While I believed everything he said to be true, the way he glanced off into the distance made me wonder if there might be something else he was holding back.

I wrinkled my nose. "So, you're telling me you have everything you've ever wanted and you're not even thirty yet?"

Mitchell didn't look at me. "You say it like it's a bad thing."

"No, but you sound so put together for someone only a few years older than me. Like, you wouldn't change anything?"

"You know," he said, looking at me over Lucas' head, "I thought you were shy."

Shy was not the word that most people in high school used. Snobby, bitchy, and rude were the ones I heard most. It surprised me that someone saw me as shy instead of stuck-up, especially Mitchell.

"You're so quiet," he added.

"I'd say I'm more anti-social than shy," I admitted.

Mitchell smirked at me and said, "You're not the girl I remember."

"Is that a bad thing?" I asked, looking up at him.

"No, not at all," he said.

In another place, with another person, at another time, I might have said something clever in return, something dripping with innuendo, but I couldn't do it. Mitchell was Lucas' friend. I was in Nine Pines. In December, I would give up everything to return to town and even flirting with Mitchell would end up complicating things. I didn't need to make the situation any harder on myself than it would already be.

I wanted to live my life while I could. I wanted to take advantage of the remaining months before I had to return back to my hometown. I'd have to get a nine-to-five, go home to make sure my parents were eating well and the bills were paid. I wanted to have some fun, to be carefree before I had to buckle down or pull up my socks or whatever the idioms were that said I had to get my shit together.

I braced myself to ruin the moment between us. Instead of taking the compliment, I needed to find a way to brush it off. Before I could say anything to sabotage the moment myself, Lucas wiggled out from between Mitchell and I.

"I'm going to puke," he shouted as he launched himself onto the front lawn of my parents' house. He landed on all fours only seconds before he vomited onto the grass and leaves. We stood there, looking away, as my brother emptied the contents of his stomach onto the lawn. Neither of us said anything over his retching.

When he stopped, I brought my shoulders to my ears and said, "I guess I better get him inside."

"I can help you if you want," Mitchell offered as he reached down and hauled Lucas to his feet.

If anyone saw Mitchell going inside our house, they wouldn't wait around to find out if he left. Before dawn, we would be the primary subject of the town gossip. Then I would have to deal with my father's disappointed looks and my mother's questions about birth control. There was no doubt they would believe the town gossip even if I told them nothing happened.

"We're good," I said, taking Lucas' arm from Mitchell.

"I already feel better," Lucas grumbled with a salute before spitting on the ground.

I cringed and told him to get into the house. As he stumbled toward the front door, I took a few steps back onto the property. "Thanks for walking us home."

Mitchell rubbed the back of his neck. I could see his muscles bulging through the sleeves of his jacket. He looked me right in the eye when he said, "Thank you for the Manhattans."

"Any time."

"I might hold you to that." He winked.

I smiled but kept backing up toward the house. If there was ever a moment to see if Mitchell was interested, that was it. I could simply suggest we get more drinks at his place. It would be easy to imply I wasn't tired. I could do anything other than backing away toward my parents' house and then I would know for sure.

I kept backing away.

"I guess I'll see you around," I said before I could change my mind.

Mitchell raised a hand and watched me go. I turned and headed to the door, where Lucas was trying to figure out which key would get him inside. When I climbed the steps and took the keys from his hand, I glanced back. Mitchell was still standing in the spotlight from the street light. I gave him a wave before pushing the house door open.

"What was that?" Lucas asked as he struggled to take off his shoes, using the wall to keep himself standing.

"What was what?" I tried to keep my voice low despite Lucas' raised voice. I put my shoes in the closet as I waited for him to form words.

"Were you hitting on Mitchell?" Lucas slurred his words. The smell of alcohol was strong on his breath.

I turned my face away. "No."

"Mitchell doesn't date girls. Just sleeps with them and leaves."

"I've heard."

"You're better than that." Lucas gave up trying to stand on one foot and sat on the ground to take off his shoes.

"What if that's what I want? Just one night of fun or whatever?" I didn't know what I expected Lucas to say, but I felt like I needed to defend myself, like I needed to prove that I could be one of those girls.

He stared up at me with tiny pupils and glassy eyes. "If I really thought that's what you wanted, I wouldn't say anything."

I redirected my attention to a painting of a deer hanging over the table near the front door while thinking about how to respond. My brother and I had always been close, but things had changed since I'd left for school. I'd grown a lot and from what I could tell, he'd stayed mostly the same. He hadn't left town. He hadn't gone to school. He still hung out with all the people he knew from high school.

"You just have all these plans. I don't want you to mess them up because of Mitchell Rizzo. Sure, he's hot, but all he's ever cared about is getting famous." Lucas' words were clear for the first time since we left the bar. "I would hate to see you get trampled in the process, or whatever."

I reached down to where Lucas was sitting and kissed the top of his head. "Thanks, big brother."

"Don't get mushy. Get me a bucket or something instead, would ya?"

I didn't wait for him to get up before I went to the kitchen to find the bucket we used for moments like those. It had no real purpose other than cleaning up messes like flooded basements, leaks in the roof, and vomit.

By the time I located it and brought it out, Lucas had moved to the living room couch and had passed out with his face hanging off the cushion. I set the bucket down on the floor beside him and went up to bed, trying not to think about what it would have been like to kiss Mitchell on my parents' front lawn. I'd allowed myself to pass up the chance to make all my teenage dreams come true.

7

———————

MITCHELL

INSTEAD OF DRIVING FROM MY MOM'S HOUSE TO THE TAILORS, I decided to walk there. I'd spent the morning waiting for my mom to come by for breakfast like she promised. I'd gotten up early and cut up fruit even though my gut told me she would stay at her boyfriend's that morning. Almost an hour after our plans, I got a text letting me know she'd slept in and would have to reschedule.

I came out of the shop with the suit in a zipped bag and detailed stories about what I'd missed when the rest of the wedding party showed up the previous weekend. Apparently, my father had brought a bottle of Jack Daniels along with them so they could make an afternoon of it. According to Mr. Perry, the tailor, it had been one of the best days he'd had since his wife passed.

To push down the feelings of missing out, I headed toward one of my favourite places in town. Music was my coping mechanism. Adding a record or two to my collection would make me feel better, and there was nowhere I would rather do that than 180 Records. It was the place I came to every time I was in town, even if that was happening less and less often. Stopping in front of the store, I took a picture for my social media. I enjoyed promoting independent shops whenever I could and 180 Records was the best of them.

The '0' in 180 was a massive record. They covered the window to the right of the door in fliers, old and new. It was a collection of show flyers, letting people know when bands would be in town. It had been a long time since Nine Pines had a venue, but I remembered the shows Forever July did there like it was yesterday.

When Forever July first started out, I'd dragged them back to Nine Pines several times, hoping it would make me feel more connected to my hometown. The opposite ended up being true. Each time I returned, the more distant I began to feel. The fewer faces I recognized in the crowd, the fewer people I hoped would talk to me after the gig.

I pulled the door of 180 Records open and stepped into the sound of Dead Kennedys playing through the speakers. When the owner's son, Myles, was working, there was always some classic punk spinning, and I appreciated that. I pivoted toward the counter to let him know I enjoyed the choice in music, but I noticed Charlie Whittaker sitting on it with her back to me. She had a hand on Myles' shoulder.

The way they were looking at each other, it was obvious I was interrupting a moment between them. Likely an intimate one.

Charlie and Myles made sense to me as a couple. They were part of the same small group of friends in high school. The group had included Hazel and two other guys whose names I couldn't remember. They were an insular group who rarely went to parties and attended all the art events in town. Every other member of their group left Nine Pines after graduation, but Myles stayed to work at the store with his dad.

Despite Myles' love for punk rock and foreign films, the kid was as small town as they came. In the few conversations I had with him, I knew he had no intention of leaving Nine Pines.

He and his dad were super close. The store was his life and he didn't want anything else. Unlike the rest of us, Myles had no reason to leave. Especially if Charlie was coming back to town.

"You sure?" Myles asked Charlie.

"Of course. Go. Have a nap or just watch TV. I've got the store today," she told him. Her voice was in a whisper, but I was close enough to hear. When I realized neither of them noticed my entrance, I turned and made my way toward the bins of records, wanting them to have their space until Charlie and I were ready to acknowledge each other.

It wasn't until Myles headed into the back room and the door closed that I heard Charlie's footsteps on the ground. I draped my garment bag over one of the many bins and began flipping through another, looking for any album that might grab my attention for that afternoon, something I could use on my old turntable at my mom's.

Without saying anything, Charlotte moved into a spot next to me, reaching up to clean the shelf above the bins. In my peripheral, I could see her standing on her tip-toes to reach the albums with the dusting brush.

"How was Lucas yesterday morning?" I asked, not taking my eyes off of the albums in front of me. My fingers kept flipping through each of them, even though I didn't actually take in any of their covers.

"Rough, but it meant he actually stuck around all morning. Got to hang out with my brother, so it was kinda cool." She stopped dusting and rested her hip against one of the wooden crates that held the records. "What do you want to listen to? I'm gonna change up the music."

I thought of six bands I could listen to that would fit my mood, but finding out Charlie's choice intrigued me.

"Whatever you're in the mood for," I told her. I pulled out an album and pretended to read the track list while she left to change the music. I set it back down as the sound of The

Head and the Heart played through the speakers. I nodded my head in appreciation.

"So, you approve?" She asked, returning to keep dusting next to me.

"I am a fan."

"Really? I thought you were only into bands like Paramore, The Flatliners, and Green Day. Or at least stuff like that." She raised both eyebrows as she waited for my response.

"I like them, but I don't like *only* them."

"Fair enough. Are you going to see The Head and the Heart in Toronto next month?" She asked as she took down a limited-edition Rancid album in a case to dust it.

"That's the plan. As long as nothing comes up with the band. I assume you're going too?"

"It's sold out, but I'm saving up for resale tickets. They're crazy expensive and I hate buying resale tickets, but…" She stared up at the ceiling like she was lost in thought. "I missed them last time because I couldn't afford to take the day off work."

"Is that why you're working here today?" I asked her.

The wistful look disappeared from her face. She glanced toward the door to the storage room and then back at me. It was as if she was deciding if she could tell me a secret. It wasn't the gossip that grabbed my attention, but the idea of sharing something with her that caused me to stand up straighter.

"Myles hasn't had a day off since his dad died. Hazel was here this morning to help out, but she had to go back to Toronto, so I'm using this weekend to contribute as much as possible." Her eyes became watery.

"Oh, shit. That sucks. I'm really sorry to hear that." I remembered when Chase lost his brother. It was impossible not to worry about my best friend, but I didn't have a clue how to help or how to make him feel better. Seeing Charlie's attitude toward helping her friend was admirable.

"Yeah, and Jorge used to let us hang out here like all the time and he put up with our childish antics, so it's the least I can do, you know? I have the week off before exams start next Monday, so I might as well put my time to good use." Despite the volume of the music, she kept her voice low. Her eyes kept darting toward the door, making sure Myles didn't come back mid-conversation.

"That's nice of you."

She shook her head. "Nah, it's not nice. It's just the right thing to do."

"You do a lot of stuff for other people, huh?" I wondered if the question was too forward. We didn't know each other and maybe it would be considered prying, but the words were out there. I couldn't do anything about that now.

To my relief, she didn't seem that worried about it. "Yeah, of course. They're family."

Nothing would make me come back to that town permanently. Unlike Charlie, I would do anything to stay in Toronto. Even thinking about settling down in Nine Pines again made my skin itchy. I decided I didn't want to talk or think about life in Nine Pines anymore.

"So, you and I are walking down the aisle together on Saturday That's cool." I watched her, gauging her reaction. I wondered if she would smile or blush.

Charlie did neither. "I'm surprised Tomas didn't make you the best man."

The lack of a reaction might have thrown me, but it was her statement that really knocked me off my game. I swallowed hard before answering her. "We're not close."

"Maybe this wedding will bring you two closer."

I tapped my fingers on the edge of the wooden bin. "I doubt it."

"That sucks," she said as she struggled to put the Rancid record back on the shelf.

Taking it from her hand, I placed it back for her. "It doesn't, really. We've never been close."

"Thanks." She nodded to the record. "Well, maybe now that he's planning to stay in Nine Pines, you can have your chance. If you want it, I mean."

I realized my mouth was agape, but I needed a moment a process what she's said. It was the first I heard about Tomas staying in town. "What?"

She tilted her head at me and asked, "*What*, what?"

"They're staying in town? I thought Tomas and Gillian were going to move back out west after the wedding. My brother was all about Vancouver Island being *life*." I put the last word in air quotes.

My brother had always wanted to live in British Columbia. Going to school in Victoria hooked him. He said he couldn't see himself living anywhere else. He loved being able to mountain bike, surf, and hike; things he once told me he couldn't do here. Yet, he was getting married and staying in Nine Pines. That wasn't supposed to be a part of the plan.

"I could be wrong," Charlie said. The phone rang across the store. She looked torn, like she might stay and keep speaking with me, but on the second ring, she spun on her heel and rushed back to the front counter.

Anger pulsed through me. Tomas was giving up everything he wanted to stay in Nine Pines. I thought about taking my phone from my pocket to text him and ask why the hell he would give up anything for that town. It made little sense. That town had nothing to offer us.

I picked up my garment bag and headed toward the door. When Charlie turned, I gave her a wave before pushing my way outside. The misty air did nothing to cool my mood as I stomped off toward my mother's house.

8

———————

CHARLIE

After saying goodbye to Myles and locking up the store for the night, I headed home in my mom's car. The driveway was empty when I arrived, as my parents were visiting friends in the next town over. They would be back late, they told me. I entered the quiet house and couldn't remember the last time I'd been there without any other family around.

When I left Nine Pines for university, I only came back for family get-togethers and when Hazel and I had plans with our friends from high school. It had been a long time since I had time to hang around the house and I didn't know what to do with myself. I found leftovers in the kitchen, but sitting at the table alone was weird. Instead, I paced around the kitchen eating the spicy tortilla soup Myles' dad taught my mom to make before he passed.

I noticed a pile of bills on the counter, and the one on top caught my attention. It was still in the envelope or even folded over. Ordinarily I might not have snooped, but it was open and the deep red letters were hard to miss.

Overdue Payment.

The total was over six hundred dollars for internet and a cellphone. I checked my bank account. Between my primary account and savings, I had enough to cover the payment. It meant I would have to pick up a Sunday shift at the bar to make up for rent, but I could manage it. It meant being exhausted for class, which wouldn't be the first time. My parents worked so hard to keep a roof over our heads when I was growing up. Several times my parents worked two jobs so we could afford Christmas gifts or to take a camping trip somewhere.

Paying the bill meant I wouldn't be able to go to see The Head and the Heart. It had been a long time since I had the time to go see a band I loved. I spent almost every single weekend working. Assignments, group projects, and papers consumed my week days. The concert was supposed to be the one luxury I allowed myself for getting so close to the end of my university career.

I had to help, even if it meant using the money I'd saved for The Head and the Heart tickets. I set the bowl of soup on the table next to all the other bills. Losing their cell phone and internet would be a blow to them, one I didn't want them to deal with.

While I had student loans to cover tuition, my parents helped me afford groceries and textbooks by sending gift cards even if money was tight for them. On the rare occasion they drove into the city to visit, they always bought Hazel and I dinner.

It wasn't only money they helped with. When Hazel and I were deep into finals, they often came to the apartment to clean and lift our spirits. They were always a phone call away. They'd done so much that paying the bill was the least I could do.

I opened my banking app. It took less than a minute to move money around and pay the bill. Within seconds, my savings and rent money were gone.

It's worth it, I told myself as I crumpled up the bill and threw it in the trash. I hoped they would forget about the notice or at least check it online before they made the payment. If I said nothing, maybe they would assume they paid for it themselves and forgot about it.

After grabbing my tortilla soup, I headed upstairs to my room, to the comfort of my bed. If I thought missing out on a concert was bad now, it would be nothing compared to the things I would miss out on when I came back to Nine Pines for good. My focus would be on fixing up the house to make it easier for my parents to live in, while paying bills, and keeping us in the home, so they could retire.

My phone vibrated as I took another mouthful of soup. It was Gillian. I swiped to answer it and put it on speakerphone.

"Hey," I said with my mouth still full.

"You're not working tomorrow, right?"

I swallowed. "Right."

"We have a problem. A big one."

I wondered if I needed to re-work the seating chart again or if a certain type of flower didn't come in for the bouquets. I took another mouthful of soup, waiting.

"The church basement is currently flooding. They haven't gotten it to stop yet, but they called to tell me they can't promise everything will be fixed and clean by Saturday. We need to find another place for the reception. And Nina, Amber, and I are going into the city tomorrow, so we can't take time to look at venues. We have appointments that we just can't miss."

The comment about Amber and Nina made me wonder what could be so important, but I tried not to focus on it too much. It was likely wedding things they needed to take care of.

Between slurps of soup, I asked, "Well, what were your options before you decided on the church basement?"

For some reason I believed it would come down to a couple choices. I assumed there would be pros and cons for each place that we could go through until we decided on which would work out best. I tried to think about all the places in town and which of them fit into their budget, but I came up blank.

"We don't have any other options. They were going to allow us to use the space for only five hundred dollars. No one else is going to let us use their space for that much. And what about the caterers? I can't get that money back. Any of it. I don't know what I'm supposed to do. I've checked everywhere, and everything is too expensive." Gillian's voice was getting higher with every word.

"Let me see if there's something I can find. What's your max budget?"

"Maybe six or seven hundred dollars. But I've checked everywhere in town."

I held the phone away from my ear. She was basically screaming through it. I set my bowl and spoon on my nightstand and said, "Give me to the end of the day tomorrow to figure something out. I'll borrow my mom's car and drive around to see some places."

"Thank you so much. I've just got so many things going on. This is the last thing I need right now."

"Not a problem. I'll start researching now."

After a few more minutes of consoling Gillian, we ended the call. I flopped back onto my bed and opened up a web browser. If I made a list of places to check out that night, maybe I wouldn't have to spend the entire day driving around, hoping to stumble onto places to hold the reception.

ARMED WITH COFFEE AND MY SECOND PIECE OF TOAST, I HEADED out the front door at eight o'clock in the morning. My online search left me with no answers, because far too many of our local businesses were without a website. I decided to drive to the nearby towns to look for churches or community centres. I pulled the door to the house shut behind me and turned with the toast in my mouth. Walking down the street was Mitchell.

He was wearing a hoodie under his jean jacket and his hair was messy, but in the way that appeared intentional. I wondered if he'd gotten up and prepared himself for the day or if he was doing the walk of shame, returning after a late night somewhere else. The latter seemed more likely from what I continued to hear about Mitchell.

He raised his hand in greeting and said, "Where are you running off to so early?"

Of course, I run into Mitchell while I had no make-up on and a piece of toast hanging from my mouth, I thought to myself as I waved back. He'd run off so fast from the store the day before, I wasn't sure if something happened or if I'd said something wrong. To make it more awkward, I currently looked like I'd just woken up while he looked like he hadn't yet gone to bed, but in a good, kind of sexy way.

I took the toast from my mouth as I stepped down onto the walkway. "I gotta look for a reception venue because of the church thing."

He stopped walking. "Church thing?"

I wondered if Tomas hadn't told him or if he'd been too busy to answer the calls.

"The church flooded. They said it won't be usable by Saturday," I explained to him. I stuck the toast back into my mouth to fish the my keys from my pocket. When I unlocked the car door and removed the toast again, I asked, "Any venue suggestions?"

He shook his head. "No. None."

"Wish me luck then."

"Hey," Mitchell said, turning up the driveway toward me. "Do you want some company?"

A little jolt of excitement hit me in the chest. Even if I didn't want to admit it, there were some residual feelings left over from that high school crush. Spending time with Mitchell was my teenage self's dream. It also seemed to be something my adult self was up for.

"You're not on your way somewhere?" I asked him.

He shook his head. "Couldn't sleep. I was just wandering and decided to see if my grandma wanted some company."

I nodded toward the passenger side of the car while reaching down to unlock all the doors. Mitchell didn't wait for verbal confirmation and climbed in before I finished my toast and did the same.

Once we'd belted in and I was backing the car out of the driveway, Mitchell asked, "Why are you the one in charge of this? It sounds like something the maid of honour could do. Or should do."

"Gillian, Nina, and Amber have appointments or something. I'm on reading week, so I have no excuse for why I can't do it," I told him. I didn't want to tell him it was just a warm-up for all the things I would have to do once I returned to Nine Pines in December. It was like that almost every time I came home. If it wasn't Gillian's wedding, I would help my mother empty the basement so a man could come check the foundation or I would end up calling insurance to make sure they were going to cover the repairs for water damage when ice damming caused a leak in the roof.

"My brother didn't even text me to tell me there was an issue with the church," Mitchell said, sitting back in his seat. I glanced at him as I turned a corner and spotted the muscles in his sharp jaw moving. He was uncomfortable or hurt. I didn't know which.

In an attempt to make him feel better, I said, "I think Gillian made the calls last night and I have a feeling I was the only one she reached out to."

"Just thought that might be something my brother would tell me since I'm also in the wedding party." He focused his attention out the passenger side window. "And I'm his damn brother."

I didn't know what to say to that or what would make him feel better about the situation. I wondered if that's why Mitchell rarely came home for the holidays or ever. The rumour was he'd left because his career was more important to him than his family, but I wondered if he left because he was unwanted. Or at least he felt that way. It was hard to imagine since every time I ran into his parents, they told me that Mitchell was living in Toronto too and that his band was getting famous and that he was actually on television and in music publications. They seemed so proud. I didn't know what to think.

"You should tell him it bothers you," I suggested as I turned onto Main Street.

Mitchell rested his head against the seat's head rest and he said, "I don't think we're those kinda people. Not him and definitely not me either."

"What kind of people?"

"The kind who talk out their problems."

"Do you want to be?" I asked, because I didn't know what else to say to him. I didn't know Mitchell well, or really at all, but sensed he was telling me things he didn't always like to talk about. Being back in Nine Pines brought up a lot of things I could push away when I was in the city. It wouldn't have been a stretch to assume it was doing the same for him.

He shifted in his seat so he could look at me. I tried to keep my eyes on the road, but I stole quick glances at him from time to time.

"I don't know." He sighed. "I guess I should figure that out, huh?"

"It might be a good start," I said.

He reached out and gave my knee a squeeze. "Thanks for being rational."

I was glad I'd stopped at a light at that exact moment,

because I couldn't focus on the road for several seconds. The touch was so brief, and it seemed so easy, so casual for him. For me, it was something else. I shifted in the seat, trying to focus on driving and not the fact that Mitchell Rizzo had just touched my leg.

"Light's green," he said.

I laughed to myself as I took my foot off the brake.

9

———————

MITCHELL

TWO TOWNS AND WE WERE NO CLOSER TO FINDING AN alternative that my brother and his fiancé could afford. Even stretching Tomas and Gillian's budget meant we'd all be crammed into small spaces for hours on end. The only place we found was further out than we would have liked. When I called around to see if there were any buses or even large vans available to haul people back to Nine Pines after a night of drinking, we were told we were out of luck. It was too last minute to be making arrangements of that size.

We stopped at a burger place only a few kilometers from Nine Pines' town limits. Despite the numerous seats inside, Charlie asked to sit outside under a massive maple tree. A red leaf drifted down and landed on my fries as we ate. I moved it to the centre of the table so we could both stare at its brilliant colour.

"Well, if anything, it was nice to take a drive today, see all the fall colours." Charlie dipped a fry in ketchup before popping it into her mouth. My eyes found a small freckle just above her lip that I hadn't noticed before. I caught myself staring at it before dipping my chin toward my food.

"It's weird that we haven't run into each other in the city," I said. "I see Hazel at shows sometimes, but never you."

"Yeah, she told me. She's my roommate, if you didn't know." Charlie bit into her burger and laughed as a tomato slipped out of the bun and onto the tray.

I handed her a napkin. "You don't go to shows with her?"

Once she swallowed, she shook her head. "Not my scene, really. I'm more into indie folk and indie rock. Mostly more mellow stuff though. Nothing against your genre at all though. I like a lot of stuff, but working at the bar every weekend only gives me time for a few events, so I go see what I love, not like."

"That must make dating hard," I said before I could stop myself. I sucked in a breath and went on, "Working evenings and weekends and all that."

She was cute. It was hard not to flirt. I needed to keep myself in check, to remember that getting involved with Lucas' sister would only be drama and it would ruin the good, chaos free thing I'd worked so hard to build.

She almost choked on her food and laughed. "Casual dating is easy. Guys tend to like that I'm busy on the weekends, so they can do whatever they want with their friends. But serious stuff is hard. Guys think they want that freedom of weekends alone until...Until they don't. I'm sure you get it."

I tried not to smile. "It's part of why I don't make commitments to anyone. Less..."

"Heartbreak?" she asked. "Less drama?"

I nodded.

"Gets lonely sometimes, though." She swirled the ketchup around with a fry.

"I guess that'll be different for you when you move back to Nine Pines, huh?" I asked her.

Once she was back in Nine Pines, the only chance I'd have to run into her would be when I came home, which rarely happened. The thought was disappointing. I could see Charlie getting along well with my friends, especially Camila. They were both honest and didn't shy away from saying things other people wouldn't. She would fit in nicely with our group dynamic.

"Dating will be way worse when I'm back in Nine Pines," she said with a short laugh. "You know how it is. Everyone is either your cousin, dealing drugs, doing drugs, or they just generally suck."

I laughed with her. "But, what about Myles?"

She raised an eyebrow at me and said, "Myles is my friend. Only a friend. Didn't we already establish this?"

There was no sign of doubt. I liked the seriousness in her voice when she said it.

I held my hands up as a sign of surrender. "Alright, Myles is a friend."

"Plus, Myles' idea of a date is taking a girl to the bowling alley and while that's cute, I..." She stopped and stared at me.

"What?"

"What about the bowling alley?" She asked.

The progression of the conversation confused me. Was she asking me to go to the bowling alley with her? Was she thinking about going to the bowling alley with Myles? I tilted my head at her, letting her know to go on.

"What if they do a reception at the bowling alley? At Nine Pines. It won't be classy, but it would be a lot of fun and I mean, it's not that much worse than a church basement," she told me. She popped a fry into her mouth and watched me, likely waiting for my reaction.

"They have that party room and with a few decorations, it might even be better than the church basement," I offered. I didn't know if it was true, but it was the closest thing I could come up with. "Plus, bowling."

"Should we go?" Charlie asked. "Maybe we can get a good deal."

I shrugged as another leaf fell from the tree onto our table. "Why rush? Let's finish our food. We have time."

She rested back in the metal chair. "Sounds like a plan to me."

THE PARKING LOT WAS EMPTY WHEN WE ARRIVED. I WORRIED WE would have to go another day without knowing for sure if we had a venue or not. I drove while Charlie phoned Tomas and Gillian and tried to convince them that it was a good idea to have the event there. They could have dinner in the event room, the place had a liquor license, and they had the space they needed. When they finally agreed, it came down to one thing: the budget.

"I know the owner, so maybe he'll cut me a deal," Charlie said as we climbed out of her parents' car. She pulled her hair back into a messy bun, like she was getting ready for battle. My eyes drifted down the length of her exposed neck. She was so pale I wondered if her veins were visible through her skin.

"I'll follow your lead," I told her, holding the door wide so she could walk ahead of me.

It was dark in the bowling alley, with no visible windows anywhere. It took my eyes several seconds to adjust and see the carpet in the distance, black with multi-coloured stars and planets. There were lanes on both sides of the building. It was dimly lit, with colourful splashes of paint on the walls and black lights to illuminate them. Despite the out-dated vibe of the place, like the wood paneling around the front desk, the bowling alley was really clean and smelled like popcorn.

I hadn't been inside Nine Pins since I was a kid. My tenth birthday party was the last time, when my parents surprised me by inviting all the kids in my grade. I remembered the way my parents fought outside almost the whole time while they left us unattended. Everyone enjoyed themselves, except for my brother and I. Tomas sat at one table for the whole time and when I'd asked him to come bowl, he'd yelled at me and told me to leave him alone. I'd spent the rest of the birthday with my friends while my family was too busy combusting.

"Can I take a look at the event room?" I asked. The elderly man behind the counter nodded and tipped his head to the double doors behind him. As I sauntered toward the double doors, I could hear Charlie explaining what they had in mind for the event, what they could bring, and what they would need.

The room was just like I remembered it. All faux wood paneling and fluorescent lighting. There were tables set up that would have to go if we were going to make the space work. I took pictures from all corners of the room and sent it to Camila, asking how to make the place look decent for a wedding reception.

Camila was one of the people I trusted most for the truth. Not only was she my best friend, but she had an eye for pinpointing beauty in things no one else might see. It was obvious in her work as a photographer and that's why I'd hired her as Tomas and Gillian's wedding photographer. She was my wedding gift to them.

Her response came in segmented messages:

panels of fabric on the walls

fairy lights behind them where the wedding party table would go

distraction pieces, like pictures or a photo booth area

She was right. It would take some work, but with a few online orders with rushed delivery, it wouldn't cost too much to get it done. Maybe my brother could finally have a good time at the bowling alley. He could replace the sour memories with good ones.

I wondered if I would be able to as well.

I headed back out to tell Charlie the ideas Camila had given me, but she was shaking her head.

"That's fair. You have a business to run," she said, leaning on the counter.

"I can't justify using the whole place for that much, especially for the whole night."

I approached, stepping into place next to Charlie. "What's wrong?"

"It would cost us twice the budget to rent out the whole place for the night and then we'd have to pay for alcohol at the bar too," she said. "But I think they already put some money down for alcohol. They can't really afford this."

Charlie pulled at her hair, making the bun tighter. Her eyes were on the wall of shoes behind the cash, but they were unfocused. I assumed she was trying to think of all the ways she could make it work. She'd already sacrificed her time for Gillian and Tomas. I didn't want her trying to think up other ways to spend her money or time for them.

"Let me call them," I said. I took my phone back out of my pocket and called Tomas. He answered on the second ring.

"What's up?" Tomas asked.

"I'm at Nine Pins with Charlie."

"Charlie Whittaker?"

"Yeah, we've been out looking for venues. It's gonna cost us twice as much to rent it out for the night than the church and we'd still have to pay for any drinks."

"Shit," Tomas muttered. The voices in the background made me wonder if he was spending time with his other groomsmen. I wondered if our father happened to be there too.

"If I pay for the space, can you guys work something out for the drinks?" I asked. Charlie stared at me, one corner of her mouth tugging up into a smile. The way she watched me gave me a sense of pride.

Tomas was quiet on the phone for a few seconds and then he said, "You already paid for the photographer."

"It's fine."

"It's a lot of money, Mitch."

"I've been told this is the kinda thing that families do for each other though, so if you can swing the booze, I'll get the space."

Charlie reached out and gave my arm a squeeze.

Tomas let out a sigh that I took for relief.

"Is it a go then?" I asked.

"Yeah, we can cancel the booze order. We'll lose the deposit, but it's still better than not having a reception at all."

"And if you need help with that stuff, let me know."

"Are you feeling okay?" Tomas chuckled.

"Yeah, why?"

"This isn't like you, that's all. Throwing money at things, sure, but usually you avoid this kinda shit. I'm not complaining though."

"I just don't want to spend all week looking for a place, alright?" I guffawed. "I'll book the place for you, okay?"

"Go for it. Talk to you soon, little brother."

After putting my phone back into my pocket, I said, "Alright, we'll take this place for Saturday."

Charlie beamed as I paid and wrote down the details for the owner, Seymour. He made us a deal to get into the space ahead of time to make it our own. Since he didn't have the event room booked for that Friday, we would be able to get in there Thursday night and all of Friday to get the place ready. He would allow us to store stuff in the room as well. I was certain he only agreed to it because Charlie promised him she would visit when she was back at Christmas.

When we headed back out to the car, Charlie nudged me and said, "That was really nice of you to do."

"Ah, it's cool. Anything to help out."

She grinned at me and it made me feel good, like she

understood that I'd stepped out of my comfort zone. There was a possibility that it meant nothing to Tomas, but I was impressed by the effort I'd made.

It turned out to be a good day and I knew a lot of that had to do with Charlie. There was a simplicity in driving around small towns and eating burgers from a diner. I enjoyed being in her company, because she didn't care about the band or that I lived in Toronto or that I had enough money to be comfortable. She seemed to be looking for someone to pass the time with while in our hometown, and it was exactly what we both needed. A friendship of convenience.

When she dropped me off at my mom's, I got her number and sent her mine.

"Text me if you're bored. We can always get a drink or coffee or something," I said as I climbed out of the car.

She gave a wave and said, "Thanks for the nice day."

"You too."

I watched her drive away before turning toward my mom's house. Even without going inside, I could tell it was empty. I stared at it, wondering if I could call Charlie to come back. I could make up some excuse about needing someone's opinion on things to get to decorate the event room. Despite all the people in town who would show up if I called, she was the only one I wanted to hang out with.

My phone rang, jolting me out of my thoughts.

"Hey."

"How's Nine Pines? How's being at home?" Chase asked. Hearing my best friend's voice made me forget about the empty house and the fact my mother hadn't even attempted to call me. He and the rest of Forever July had that effect on me.

"Calling it home is a bit of a stretch, but it's fine. Nothing changes here," I told him with a laugh as I pulled my keys from my belt.

To Chase, home was where his family was. His understanding of my situation was surface level. I don't think he fully grasped that he, Camila, and the band were my family.

Though not by blood, Chase was my brother in every way that counted. I could tell him everything. He wouldn't judge me, he would always be there for me, and I realized I'd let him down. I'd been so caught up with family and Charlie that I hadn't checked out the documents Chase posted in the band chat. I hadn't even touched my guitar since getting to town.

"I'm surprised I haven't heard from you about those rough lyrics I sent over. I wanted to hear what vibe you thought we should go with."

"Shit. Sorry, man." I told him. "I'm going to get to them right now." I pushed the door open and stepped into the house.

"Is everything okay? You sound kinda on edge. Have you slept? I know you've been feeling kinda beat down lately, so if you wanna wait and..."

"Nah, I'm good, honestly. Some wedding stuff came up, but it should be smooth sailing from here on out," I told him, hoping he would drop the conversation. Chase knew enough about my family to ask about how it was going.

"You sure you're doing all right? Camila told me you weren't sleeping and Mo said you were feeling like shit," Chase said. "We've all been worried about you."

Chase, Mo, and Camila had been talking about me. It shouldn't have surprised me that they had been discussing my mental health, but it annoyed me a bit. I wondered if they sat around at the jam hall talking about me when I wasn't there last night.

"I'm getting sleep," I told him. "I'll be back to my old self when we can hit the road again. I'm getting restless."

I'd been restless since the day we returned home.

"Me too," Chase said. "That's why I'm writing so much."

I headed straight into the basement where I used to jam

before I left town. "And I'm back at the house now, so I'm going to check out the lyrics and send you some riffs in a bit."

"Promise me you're good?"

I laughed. "Dude, I'm good."

"I know family stuff is tough for you and I want you to know I'll be here to vent if you need it, cool?"

Chase never let me down. He never left me when I needed him. He and Camila were the rocks in my life and I loved them for that.

"I know, dude. Thanks." I swallowed hard. "I'm gonna start playing right this second, cool?"

Chase let me know Forever July were planning another jam session and if I wanted to video call just to let them know and they would set it up. He would keep me updated in our group chat. I told him I was down with whatever and settled into the bean bag chair that had been there since I was fifteen.

There was something about the exposed concrete and beams above my head that put me in the head space for making music. Even though my mom wasn't home from her boyfriend's place, even though I wouldn't disturb someone else in the house, I stayed there. I grabbed my acoustic guitar from its stand and set it in my lap.

With my fingers on the strings, I realized how much time I'd wasted running around all day, doing stuff for a brother who almost forgot to invite me to his bachelor party. I'd also been the one to suggest we didn't need to rush when Charlie suggested the bowling alley. I'd gotten so caught up in things in Nine Pines, I allowed myself to slip.

I'd put the band on the back burner and for what?

If I wasn't careful, I'd end up like my parents, bitter at the world because their dreams never came true.

10

———

CHARLIE

Such a good day, I thought to myself. I headed into the house, ready to tell my parents all about what we accomplished in one afternoon. It occurred to me that I should hold back how everything had been done in the company of Mitchell Rizzo. The whole thing had been innocent, but something about it made me question if it should remain a secret. Especially when he'd put his phone number into my contact list. I bit the inside of my cheek to keep from smiling.

Mitchell turned out to be nicer than I assumed he would be. He was good looking, sure, and from what I was told he didn't struggle for women's attention, but part of me always assumed he would treat me like other men had in the past. They were nice when they wanted to sleep with me and then if it wasn't working out, they turned into entitled assholes.

Mitchell had made no moves that suggested he was interested in sleeping with me. At least none that I had picked up on. From what I could tell, he saw me as nothing more than someone to pass the time in Nine Pines with. I had no reason to pass that up. While Hazel was in Toronto during the week and Myles was working all the time, Mitchell could keep me company. It was definitely better than the other people I heard were back in town for the study break.

"Charlotte," my brother said, appearing in the hallway as I hung my bag and sweater on the wall hooks.

"Oh, hey, what are you doing here?" I asked.

"Thought I would come by and have dinner here before the thing happening at Tyson's tonight. He's back from college, so he invited some people around." Lucas leaned against the wall as I took my shoes off. "You coming?"

"Yeah, sure. I'm not working until ten tomorrow, so I can come by for a bit."

"You going to invite Mitchell?" Lucas asked.

My head shot up and, at the sight of my brother's face, my brows furrowed. Lucas' eyes were staring right into mine. Despite his straight face, I could sense the *gotcha!* moment brewing.

"I heard you two were hanging out all day." One of his eyebrows arched. The corner of his mouth twitched.

And there it was.

"We were just doing wedding stuff," I said as I headed toward the kitchen. "Gillian asked us to help her find a reception venue."

My parents were cooking together, wearing matching red and white checkered aprons my mom made when Lucas and I were young. I gave them both kisses on the cheek and asked if I could do anything to help out.

"If you two could set the table, that would be great," my dad said. I tried not to stare at him too long as I checked his posture and the dark pouches beneath his eyes. I didn't want him to notice I was checking for signs of exhaustion. When I was in Nine Pines for a weekend a while ago, I'd overheard my mom telling a friend about a part-time job he was thinking about applying for.

He looked the same as always. Maybe a little softer around the edges, but still my dad.

Lucas hovered as I grabbed the cutlery and headed into the dining room. Without being asked, he grabbed place mats from our grandmother's old hutch and put them in our regular spots. I walked behind him, setting the cutlery down.

"If you're hoping Mitchell is going to stop sleeping around to be with you, you're wrong," Lucas hissed. We both glanced toward the kitchen to see if our parents were aware of our conversations. They continued to talk amongst themselves, chatting and grinning at each other. Lucas leaned toward me and said, "He's basically a rockstar. He's not going to give up that life for you. You aren't the exception to the rule."

"First of all, he's not a rockstar." I rolled my eyes. "He's just some guy in a band. And secondly, I'm not trying to date Mitchell."

While it might be an understatement of Mitchell's abilities, calling him a rockstar was overstating it too. Mitchell was successful. He had fans, lots of them.

Lucas got one thing right. Mitchell wasn't going to give up his lifestyle to be with anyone. What Lucas seemed to forget is that I had plans of my own that I wouldn't be able to let go of.

"You're fine with being some gross hook up?"

"Just stop, Lucas. I'm not trying to hook up with anyone. Mitchell and I were hanging out *doing wedding stuff*. Unlike you."

"Oh please," Lucas rolled his eyes as he tossed the last mat onto the table, ignoring the dig about him being useless when it came to the wedding. "I saw the way you looked at him that night at the bar. Every time you gave him a drink, you were basically undressing him."

"That's what I do with everyone. Guys and girls," I hissed at him. "That's how I get tips, dumbass."

"No, he's different. I saw it with my own eyes."

He wasn't wrong, but I wasn't going to admit that to him.

"You were so messed up, you don't know what you saw." I stormed back into the kitchen and grabbed cups from the cupboard. Lucas was right behind me, taking the jug of water from the fridge. As I slammed each glass onto the table, Lucas filled it.

"Everyone is talking about the two of you," Lucas said. "It's embarrassing."

"What's embarrassing is how much people in this stupid town gossip and make up ridiculous things in their heads just because they're bored with their own lives." I put the last cup down with a thud and stared at him, hands on my hips. "Don't make assumptions about me, Lucas. I've never made assumptions about you and what you're up to, despite all the rumours I hear."

Lucas stared at me. His eyes went from narrow to wide. From his reaction, it was obvious I'd struck a nerve. It made me worried that what people were saying about my brother was true. I didn't want to believe he got himself mixed up with the crowd of burn outs in town. I didn't want to think that he was getting involved with drugs, but the way he turned from the door and stalked off, it said more than any of the rumours had.

"What happened?" My mother asked, stepping into the dining room.

"We got into a disagreement." I met my mom's eyes and asked in a whisper, "Is he doing okay?"

At one time, Lucas and I had been close. We told each other secrets and complained about our parents together. He'd invite me to hang out with him and his friends without worrying what they might think. If I hadn't moved away, I would have known all the details of what was going on with him, but each year I spent living in the city, the more distance it put between us emotionally.

Her head shake was long and slow. "He doesn't talk to us,

but I think it's safe to assume he isn't happy with the way his life is going right now."

I sat down in one of the dining room chairs and thought about what Lucas had said. The gossip was already swirling. I missed the city, how I could do anything I wanted without being 'found out'. There was barely a friendship with Mitchell and I and it frustrated me to know that people were making more out of it than it was.

I was determined to prove them wrong. Nothing would happen between Mitchell and I.

IF I CLOSED MY EYES AND PRETENDED THAT IT WASN'T COUNTRY music playing, I could almost believe we were at a house party in Toronto. I determined, if I had a few more drinks, the music would start sounding better to me. It had happened before. Most of the people at the party were younger than me, kids who left recently to go to school. It wasn't unusual for there to be get-togethers during reading week when people returned, but what I didn't expect was the size of it. It wasn't just a hangout, but a full party on a Sunday night.

At one point, it had been only Myles and I in the kitchen, ignoring everyone and chatting about anything and nothing. Lucas disappeared with some guys I made a point of not talking to, and I'd assumed they were out back smoking weed as they often did. As the party grew, I started scanning the space for Mitchell. Besides Myles, he was the only other person in town I wanted to talk to. It was weird to think that only two days before I had yet to speak a full sentence in front of him. It would be nice for him to join Myles and I that night, but he didn't walk through the door and after more than a few drinks, I stopped checking. I ended up dancing with some friends I went to high school with. We'd lost touch when we left town for different university and colleges, but once the alcohol warmed me up, the awkwardness between us all melted. I showed off some bar tricks in the kitchen when a guy a few years younger than me said he could make more tips as a bartender than me if he tried.

It might have only been midnight, but I was still mostly sober and ready to leave the party. I glanced around, looking for Lucas. Myles nodded toward the basement door and said, "I think I saw him head downstairs. Maybe just text him that you're leaving?"

I shook my head. "I just want to let him know I'm heading out. I'll be right back."

I might not have gone looking for Lucas before leaving if I was already living in Nine Pines. Lucas and I had gone to several of the same parties while I was in high school and we never made a point of letting each other know when we were heading out for the night, but it felt like the right thing to do since we'd come together. Unlike before, I felt like a guest in town, so I made my way toward the basement. I stopped halfway down the stairs, unsure of what to do with what I was seeing.

I'd been hearing all about it for months but I refused to believe it was true. Despite pretending the gossip was only gossip, I found Lucas cutting lines on the top of Tyson's coffee table. I stood on the carpeted stairs, watching as he snorted white powder up his nose; one line and then another. He wiped up what he missed with his pointer finger and rubbed it beneath his lips like I'd seen people do in movies.

Nausea overtook me and I gripped the stair railing to keep me steady.

If it had been a Friday or Saturday night or if he had been celebrating something in particular, I might not have been as shocked to see what I was seeing. Realizing that my brother was snorting coke on a Sunday night, a work night, hit me so hard I couldn't breathe.

There was no point in confronting him while he was high. It would lead to an argument. I climbed the stairs two at a time and headed into the backyard to get away from everyone. I slipped through the mudroom and out to the side of the house. Once out in the cold, I realized someone had built a fire near the back of the property and there were bodies huddled around it.

The vibe at fire pits was always different from the one in the house. It would be quiet, people sitting around with beers staring into the flames, maybe smoking a little marijuana. It was what I needed. The warmth and quiet would give me time to sort out my thoughts. If I went home, my parents would be awake and they would notice I was on edge. If I stayed inside Tyson's house, I wouldn't be able to keep my mouth shut. One look at Lucas and I would scold him. I could feel it coming on.

I couldn't believe my brother was exactly what people said he was. While I was gone, he'd turned into someone I didn't recognize. I'd left my family only for the bills to go unpaid and my brother to be snorting cocaine on a Sunday night. The more I thought about it the angrier I became.

Before I made it to the fire pit, someone strummed a guitar. I squinted at the orange and red faces around the fire and saw Mitchell sitting there with a guitar on his lap and his eyes focused on the woman beside him. I recognized the woman as Zara, who worked in the bakery. Her hand was on Mitchell's forearm and his eyes were on her. They were smiling at each other as he strummed a few chords that I recognized. He was playing one of his band's songs for everyone. I could hear them making recommendations. They gushed over him.

After the day we had, it surprised me he hadn't at least said hello when he arrived. I wondered if it was because I hadn't been enthusiastic about hanging out with him the way the people around the fire pit were. Maybe I didn't tell him how much I loved his music. Maybe I didn't ask for selfies to show my friends that I knew Mitchell Rizzo. Maybe I didn't stroke his ego enough.

"Ugh," I groaned as I caught myself thinking about those things. Jealousy was an ugly emotion. I didn't know what I was being jealous about and I was too drunk to figure it out. My anger with Lucas was seeping out in all directions.

Mitchell glanced away from his guitar and Zara, catching my eye. I turned back toward the house and marched toward the front of the property. There was no reason for me to stay.

I texted Myles and told him I was heading home, but to call if he wanted to stay at my place instead of making the walk back downtown.

"Charlie," Mitchell called out to me as I made it to the road. I didn't stop walking, because I was too angry with my brother and with myself. It didn't take Mitchell long to catch up. He ran in front of me and blocked my path.

"Where are you going?"

"Home."

"It's only midnight."

"Lucas is currently snorting coke in the basement on a Sunday night." The words burst out of me. Any self control I had left was gone, thanks to the alcohol. I could hear the high pitch hysteria in my voice, but I was too drunk to control it. "Like, he doesn't even want to leave Nine Pines, but he can't even help out at home. He plans on staying here forever, but I have a good thing going in Toronto and I want to be there with my friends and I can't. I have to come back here and take care of my parents. And he's in there blowing money up his nose or whatever and not helping me out."

"I think your parents can take care of themselves," Mitchell said. He reached out and put his hands on my upper arms. He gave them a squeeze. "They're adults."

He smelled like camp fire and a sweet, almost floral

cologne. I breathed it in before taking a step back and breaking his grip on me.

"My parents are struggling financially. They've done so much for me. I can't let them down."

"But you can't put your own dreams aside for someone else," Mitchell said to me. His eyes were heavy with seriousness.

A snort of a laugh came out of me. It was more sarcastic than I planned. "It's not surprising that's your take on this situation."

"What does that mean?" Mitchell asked. He folded his arms in front of him.

My mind was screaming at my mouth to stop moving, but the emotions were pulsing through me with abandon. I folded my own arms to match his. "It's easier when you're not tied down, right? Don't get too attached to anything or else you might actually have to make sacrifices for someone else."

"That's such a black and white way of looking at things," Mitchell shot back. He shook his head before saying, "If you just give up all your plans for someone else, you'll end up bitter and resentful. Clearly, you're already a little resentful."

"Yeah, and how happy are you? You've got a very resentful vibe about you too," I said, my voice getting higher.

He flinched, but he didn't take his eyes from mine.

I sucked in a breath. "I'm really sorry. I'm angry at Lucas and not you."

"I think you're a little angry at me too. Right?"

I shrugged, but then shook my head.

"I have to get back. Zara's waiting for me," Mitchell said.

I felt something in my chest tighten. The jealousy was back. Instead of opening my mouth, I nodded. Neither of us moved for a few seconds until the front door of Tyson's house opened.

"Charlie?" Myles called. "I'm heading out."

I gave Mitchell a tight-lipped smile before turning to Myles. He walked toward me with both of our coats in hand. I took mine from him and said, "Wanna come over? Watch a movie or something?"

"Yeah. I'm not ready to go home, just to leave that party," Myles said. He nodded at Mitchell and told him to have a good night.

"You too," Mitchell said to him, but his eyes were on me. Since there was nothing left to say, I walked past him toward my house.

Myles linked arms with me and whispered, "You good?"

I could have told him about my feelings of jealousy, but I decided to stick to the one that wouldn't cause the rumours to spread like wildfire. "Does everyone know Lucas has a drug problem?"

"Everyone." Myles sighed. "Sorry, Charlie. We weren't going to tell you until you came home at Christmas. We didn't see the point when you weren't here."

"You don't have to defend that decision," I said. "You had your own stuff going on. Plus, I should have noticed."

I couldn't defend my brother. Thinking about what Lucas was getting himself into made my stomach tighten. As we walked away from the house, my anger was morphing into worry. If I allowed myself to get caught up in concern, I wouldn't sleep that night.

"If it makes you feel any better, I think he still has some control over his life," Myles told me. "I think he's just kinda sad with how his life has turned out. You get that, don't you?"

We walked the rest of the way in silence.

By the time we opened the front door of my house, I regretted everything I said to Mitchell. My hurt manifested into anger and it'd done nothing to help the situation. Taking it out on him wasn't fair. I wondered if he would talk to me again before the wedding.

After grabbing us glasses of water, I curled up in my dad's Laz-E Boy. Myles took the couch. We fell asleep watching old Brooklyn Nine-Nine episodes.

11

MITCHELL

WHILE CHARLIE SAID THERE WAS NOTHING GOING ON WITH HER and Myles, they seemed to spend an awful lot of time together. They even went back to her parents' house together. Myles wasn't into men, I knew that much, so I couldn't help but wonder if they were friends with benefits. Something had to be going on.

That thought carried me back to the fire pit, to Zara and the group of kids who had been begging me to play Forever July songs, to sing the words that Chase wrote. The music was mine, but they wanted the lyrics. They wanted to relate to me through Chase's love songs. There wasn't any of me in those lyrics. I didn't think I was capable of writing a love song.

When I dropped into the deck chair, I saw my brother sitting across the fire with a beer. Tomas was telling everyone how he bought the old Wiess house on the edge of town, so they could have some land for homesteading, if that's what they decided to do.

Ignoring Tomas' decision to stay in Nine Pines, I turned my attention back to Zara. Her perfume smelled like warm sugar. She licked her lips as I reached down for the guitar between our chairs. Before I sat up, Zara ran a long finger down my sweater sleeve and said, "Guitarists always have the best arms. I bet you have strong arms."

Any other night, I would have asked right there if we were going back to my place or hers. If I were still sober, like I was in that moment, we might have hung around the party for a little longer, doing shots between making out in the hallway.

"Gilly said she wants chickens, so we're getting chickens," Tomas said to someone in the circle while he chuckled to himself. "If you want fresh eggs, you know where to come."

Tomas hated eggs. Tomas hated birds. Tomas said that he wanted to move to British Columbia, but he was giving everything up for a woman. He was going to stay in Nine Pines and become a farmer. Why? Because his fiancée wanted it?

"So, that's what Gillian wants. And what do you want?" I asked. My voice was louder than anyone else's around the fire pit.

Tomas turned to look at me through the violent movement of the flames. He tilted his head to one side and asked, "What's that, little brother?"

I sat up straighter and set the guitar back into the grass. Zara put a hand on my arm, dragging her fingers toward my elbow, but ignored it.

"What happened to moving back to B.C.? I thought you wanted to live that west coast life? Surfing, biking, and climbing." I tried to sound casual, but my voice wouldn't steady itself.

Tomas sat back in his seat and took a sip of his beer like the question amused him, almost like he'd been expecting it. After he swallowed the mouthful of beer, he said, "Things change and they have. What if we wanna have kids or something? What if someone in the family gets sick? What if we lose our jobs?"

"You can come back later," I told him. I straightened my shoulders. "Why do it now?"

All the faces, glowing in the fire light, turned their attention back and forth between us. It was a conversation for another time, I knew, but I needed the answer. I didn't understand why Tomas would want to stay in a town that held so many bad memories. I couldn't come up with a rational reason to give up on everything you dream of for another person.

Our parents had done the same thing. They fell in love. They had children. They gave up all the dreams they had. When the novelty of having kids and a family wore off, they hated each other because of all the things they'd sacrificed. They blamed their children for impeding their life goals and dreams. I didn't know why Tomas would want to put himself through that.

"I can't explain it to you, Mitch," he said. "Maybe one day you'll let yourself fall for a girl worth giving everything up for."

Zara shifted in her chair, bumping her knee against mine.

"I doubt it," I mumbled to myself as I grabbed the guitar again. I strummed a few chords before looking at Zara and asking, "Any requests?"

Zara nodded. Her lips parted to speak. Before the words came out, Tomas called out, "What's that song about living alone? That one you wrote?"

"Studio Apartment," I said. It came as a surprise to me to find Tomas knew one of my songs. He'd never been interested in my music. As much as I wanted to relish the fact he took an interest, I understood his choice. In any other conversation, I might be flattered by the suggestion, that they wanted one of my songs and not Chase's. I wasn't.

"Yeah." He laughed. "Play that one."

Earlier in the night, everyone was bickering over what Forever July song they wanted to hear. Now there was nothing but the popping and hissing coming from the fire pit. I adjusted the guitar and strummed a chord as if checking to see if it was tuned, even though I knew it was. When no one else spoke, I began to play.

in my studio apartment,
there's barely room for two
you said you can stay another night,
if i would only let you

Even as I sang, even as my fingers played the chords, I thought about Charlie. I'd be living in a studio apartment because I wanted to. Charlie was giving up everything she wanted out of her life for her family and wondered why she couldn't have the best of both worlds.

FOR SEVERAL SECONDS AFTER BLINKING OPEN MY EYES, I wondered if I'd gotten a ride back to Toronto and was waking up in my apartment. It was bright and warm, and the leaf of a Philodendron Melanochrysum hung over my face. Only when I smelled bacon did I realize where I was. I'd passed out on the floor of my grandmother's sunroom.

I winced when I remembered her finding me with one leg through her living room window.

"I've been bumping around in here for almost thirty minutes trying to wake you up," my grandma said with a snort of a laugh. "If you weren't going to get up and drink some water, I was going to start misting you like a plant."

She squeezed the spray bottle of water in my direction. I closed my eyes and let the light droplets of water cover my face and neck.

"I'll get up," I mumbled.

"There's bacon in the kitchen if you want to make yourself a BLT," she told me before walking back into the living room.

My world pulsed then tilted as I tried to stand. It took me three tries to get myself into a semi-upright position. A hangover that intense was impressive considering how hard I drank on tour while still having to perform the next night. That morning was the worst hangover I'd suffered in a long time.

I dragged myself into the living room where my grandma made herself comfortable in the chair facing the television. She had a cup of tea on the little table next to her and a piece of toast on her plate.

"You want any fruit, Grams?" I asked as I walked into the kitchen. "What about some of that bacon?"

"I have my breakfast," she said before turning up the sound of the television. I thought about arguing with her, but I went to the fridge and pulled out the strawberries and a peach that was going soft. Even the strawberries were on their last legs, but I cut them into small pieces, tossing the bad parts. It took me longer than I'd like to admit because I had to sit down twice to keep from throwing up in the sink.

With my BLT made and the fruit split between us, I took a seat on the couch to eat. As soon as my ass hit the cushion, my grandma turned off the television and shifted in her chair to get a better look at me.

"What's up, Grams?" I asked between mouthfuls of bacon and bread. "Sorry about breaking into your house last night."

"This morning."

I chuckled and followed it up by wincing. "Yes, this morning."

She reached into the deep pocket of her beige cardigan and tossed something at me. I almost dropped my plate to catch the pink key chain. It was a key. A house key.

"Just use the front door next time. Any time," she told me. She turned back to her bowl of fruit and munched on it as if the gesture wasn't immense. Maybe for other people it was a simple one, but my father hadn't given me a key to his house. My mother told me she would have one made for me 'in case of an emergency.'

"Thanks, Grandma."

"Now, tell me, are you going to apologize to the Whittaker girl or what?" She asked before popping a piece of fruit in my mouth. It came back to me. I'd ranted away to my grandma for a while about Charlie. I had no idea how long it went on. The alcohol and weed had made time fuzzy.

I rubbed the back of my neck. "I should."

"You should do it now."

"Maybe not right now." I gestured to my rumpled clothes and askew hair.

"Well, go get showered and change into something nice."

At my grandma's request, I did just that. My head might have been aching and my stomach was uneasy, but when I walked out of the house dressed in last night's clothes, no one would have noticed the agony I was in. The air was bitterly cold, but it helped me feel better almost right away. I stood a little straighter as I knocked on Charlie's door.

It was her mom that appeared in front of me. She beamed and said, "Mitchell, it's always so nice to see you. Lucas isn't here. Did he not tell you? He has a place of his own across town now."

From somewhere in the house, I heard Charlie say, "Dad, you guys can't keep taking on all these projects around the house. Let me call a plumber."

"I don't need a plumber," her father said with a loud groan. "Don't pester me. If you wanna help me, finish your master's degree and get a good-paying job so you can afford a plumber for yourself."

The comment Charlie had made the night before came back to me. She had a lot to worry about. My parents were so caught up in themselves I didn't know what drama was going on in their lives or if they even had money troubles. From how easily my mother left her house empty for days on end, I doubted they did, but I wouldn't know for sure.

"I'm sorry you have to hear this bickering," Mrs. Whittaker said with a warm smile. "I think Charlotte is under some added stress at school."

I knew it wasn't about school, but her concern for her parents' well-being.

"It's actually Charlie I'm here to see."

Mrs. Whittaker's mouth turned into a perfect O. She held up a finger and turned her back to me. "Charlotte, there's someone at the door for you."

She appeared in the front hallway wearing a pair of tight leggings and a long t-shirt. At the sight of me, she folded her arms, but it came off as awkward and not angry. When I smiled at her, she let her arms fall to her side.

"Hey," she said, taking a few steps closer. With a nod, her mom gave us space.

Charlie had twisted her hair up into a messy bun. Everything about her said *I'm hungover and owning that.* I could see she'd attempted to wash her makeup off, but there were still hints of mascara and eyeliner around her left eye. She looked cute.

"Wanna go for a coffee or something?" I asked her.

"Kind of."

"Kind of?"

"Can I go like this?" she asked, gesturing to herself. "I'm too tired to get changed."

I tried to keep my eyes from lingering too long on her shapely figure. "I'm wearing the same clothes from last night, so I'm going to say yes, please do."

While calling out to her parents that she would be back,

she grabbed a man's flannel jacket from the hooks by the door. She pulled the door shut behind her and said, "Thanks for offering to take me for breakfast. I'm way too hungover to make myself anything."

"Thanks for saying yes."

12

———

CHARLIE

IN THE CAFE, ONLY A FEW RETIREES HUNG OUT BY THE WINDOW. Everyone else was at work. All the vacationers were gone for the season. Their cottages were closed up until the spring. We stepped through the doorway and unzipped our coats, allowing in the warmth. I rubbed my hands together as we moved into the butter yellow café.

"In the back?" Mitchell asked. "Away from the sun?"

It might have been a watery sun, but it still was too bright, too much for my hungover eyes to handle. The pressure behind them made me flinch several times on our walk downtown. I nodded at his suggestion and followed him to the back of the place. We slipped into either side of the booth, facing each other. I rested my head against the wall and said, "As a bartender, you think I'd know my limit by now."

"Maybe you just needed a night to let go," Mitchell offered.

"I guess so," I said with a laugh. "I would say I got pretty wound up though. Sorry again about that."

"Nah, I shouldn't have said anything. You and I have very different family dynamics." He stood up and said, "I'll grab us some coffee."

Mitchell went up to get himself a coffee and grabbed me a breakfast sandwich and espresso at the same time. He didn't forget to grab two glasses of water for us either. We settled into quiet chat about being back in town, how weird it was seeing people that night before. It had been a strange night, hanging out with people from high school. We agreed that each time we came back, it got stranger to be there.

There was a lull in the conversation, so I asked, "Same clothes as last night. You and Zara have a good time?"

It took me a few seconds to realize how inappropriate the question was. Unlike the awkward things I said the night before, I couldn't blame my question on the alcohol. My lack of tact was embarrassing. I glanced away from Mitchell trying hard to look unfazed by the whole thing. I took in the old wooden tables and chairs around us. The rustic light fixtures hanging low over our table.

Mitchell raised a single eyebrow. "Is that a hint of jealousy I detect in your voice, Charlotte Whittaker?"

My face burned, and I was wearing no makeup to conceal it. Was it jealousy? I didn't know for sure. I shrugged and said, "Jealousy? No. I was trying to ask about your night, but it just came off kinda gross. Like, super gross."

When I wrinkled my nose in disgust with myself, he laughed and reached across the table. He put a hand on top of mine. His calloused fingers gave mine a squeeze. I froze. I feared making any sudden movements would cause his touch to end. The concern that someone would see us in the moment disappeared. I didn't care if there were rumours. His skin against mine felt amazing.

"Zara and I are just friends," Mitchell said. He removed his hand and scratched at his stubble. He never took his eyes off me and my cheeks continued to blaze.

I almost wished he would look away so I could take a second to compose myself. I tried to think of something smart or witty to say, but my brain was too overwhelmed by his touch to put together a cohesive thought. I sat back in my chair and said, "That's cool."

"You know what I did after I left Tyson's last night?"

"What did you do after you left Tyson's?" I took a sip of my water.

Instead of answering right away, he picked up the white mug of coffee and took a sip. It made me wonder if he wanted to see me squirm, if he was dragging it out to get a reaction out of me. If he waited any longer, I might have obliged.

He set the mug down, glanced around the half empty diner, and said, "I crawled in through my grandmother's window, ranted to her for who knows how long, and passed out on the floor of her sunroom."

A laugh burst out of me. At the sound, Mitchell laughed too.

"So, your grandma is your go-to person?" I asked.

He nodded. He reached across to my plate and grabbed the tomato from where I left it. After covering it in a light shake of both salt and pepper, he took a bite of it.

"That's nice," I told him. I took a sip of my espresso and said, "I barely know my grandparents. They all live far away, out east."

"My grandma and I were always close, but especially when Tomas left for college and my parents' relationship started falling apart. They sent me to live with my grandma in the eleventh grade. It was just supposed to be temporary, while they got back on their feet, but then there was the divorce and my dad moved out."

"It's nice that you had a place to go, and that you had your grandma at least."

Mitchell glanced away from me. The muscles in his jaw twitched. I set my coffee back down, ready for whatever he had to say. I thought about pushing him for an answer, but I got the feeling he was trying to figure out the best way to explain himself.

"She's great. Honestly, living with her was the most stable part of my childhood or youth or whatever." His eyes still avoided mine. "But during that time, my parents realized they could do what they wanted and be who they wanted if they didn't have kids to look after. I had bedrooms at both my mom and dad's houses, but they never knew when I was supposed to be there and never asked. At first it was cool. Then it wasn't. Only my grandma checked in on me."

There were no right words to say to something like that. It was stressful seeing my parents worry about money and there were times when it would put a strain on their relationship. Sometimes it caused arguments and general tension, but at the end of the day they would do anything for my brother and I. Even when we thought our parents might divorce after my father lost one of his jobs, Lucas and I knew that they would never let something like money or a rift in their relationship come between their children. We knew we were lucky that way.

Mitchell didn't have the luxury of stability. I no longer wondered why he avoided returning to Nine Pines, why he didn't put in the effort for his family anymore. They hadn't given him a reason to. They hadn't done the same for him.

"I'm glad you had your grandma," I told him.

"And I realized your family is really lucky to have you," he told me. He ran a hand through his dark hair and said, "I'm thinking about coming back to Nine Pines more, doing stuff for my grandma. And while I'm here, I gotta make sure she eats right and that her house is clean."

I wondered if part of that decision was affected by the conversation we'd had, the things I'd said to him. Maybe it had always been something he'd been thinking about. It was possible he needed it as much as he said his grandmother did. Mitchell was turning out to be more rounded than I expected him to be. Growing up, I always saw him as this untouchable figure. He was my older brother's best friend. He was always talking about how he was going to get out of Nine Pines, see the world, and do these big things. Then he left. It only solidified that feeling for me. He was doing everything he said he would do. He was becoming the person he said he would, but it was obvious he wasn't perfect. Our conversations put him into perspective. He was flawed, which I could see now, but it made him more real.

I smiled at him and said, "I'm sure she's really happy you're home."

"Yeah, it's nice to see her."

I paused for a few seconds, contemplating if I should ask what had been on my mind for a while. I knew it had the potential to ruin our nice moment, but I wanted to know. "Can I ask a question?"

Mitchell sat back in his seat and said, "I'm going to assume this is about the wedding?"

I nodded.

"Go ahead. I've been waiting for this, honestly."

I raised an eyebrow.

"Not from you specifically. I've just been waiting for someone to ask, so go ahead." He nodded at me, as if telling me to go on.

After a breath, I said, "I'm just curious why you decided to change your mind and come to the wedding after saying no."

"Things got rescheduled, so I got a chance to do it." The words spilled from his mouth too quickly. There was no conviction in his voice.

I blinked at him, letting him know his excuse was transparent. I wanted to push, but if he wasn't ready, there was no point. He would tell me the same thing over and over.

His phone vibrated on the table. He reached for it and flipped it over. There was an alarm set that said, "video call - band". Mitchell cursed and set the phone back down. He reached for his wallet and said, "I'm sorry. I gotta go. I totally forgot about my band practice."

From his frantic rushing to drink the remainder of his coffee, I knew better than to offer to walk back with him. I picked up my coffee and took a sip while he raised his arms to shrug on his jacket. His shirt rose up, exposing the bottom of a tattoo coming down from his rib cage. I couldn't see enough to tell what it was. He caught me looking at him and smiled at me. I grinned back.

"I'll text you," he said.

"Okay."

He turned to walk away, but stopped and pivoted back. He leaned onto the table, looking me in the eye. "Sorry to run, honestly. You've made being in Nine Pines more fun."

He didn't give me time to come up with an answer before rushing out of the cafe. I bit my bottom lip to keep from smiling too hard. Despite his quick departure, I was enjoying my time with Mitchell. It would be disappointing when the week came to an end.

Instead of leaving the cafe, I relaxed into my chair, sipping my espresso and wondering what life was going to be like in Nine Pines when I didn't have Mitchell and a week of wedding stuff distracting me.

13

MITCHELL

As I took long strides toward my mom's house, I wondered if the band was going to wait around or if they were jamming without me. Being away from them during one of our practice sessions was already going to make it strange. I'd let them down by showing up late. They responded to my apology text letting me know they were waiting, that it was cool, but I'd let them down by losing track of time.

Charlie had that effect on me.

I was sweating when I burst through the front door. I didn't bother taking off my jacket or shoes before rushing into the basement. To avoid holding my band up further, I opened my laptop, tapped on the video call app, and dropped onto the couch. *At least*, I thought to myself, *I'd left the microphone set up*. While the call connected, I slipped out of my jacket and pulled my acoustic from the stand into my lap.

The video call connected and an array of sounds filled the basement; Voices, instruments, the general humming of commotion. No one seemed to notice at first that I'd joined in on our meeting.

"Hey. I made it. What's going on?"

Chase turned and leaned into the camera. He squinted and asked, "You good? Like, are you feeling good?"

It shouldn't have surprised me that Chase was checking in on my emotional state. Even when we were both in Toronto, we rarely went a day without texting. Between my mom's empty house, helping with my grandma, and spending time with Charlie, my responses to him and my friends had been sporadic at best.

I chuckled. "Yeah. Why?"

Even before her face showed up, I could see Camila's dark curls enter the frame. She shoved her cheek next to Chase's and asked, "Are you okay?"

I should have expected Chase would have rounded up Camila to check in on me. What I didn't expect was the whole band to be there when they checked in on me. Mo and Dylan weren't even attempting to keep their voices down in the background. I wondered if Camila was at the jam hall when they got to talking about me or if she made a trip there out of concern.

"Honestly, I'm fine. What's going on?"

"You didn't text us back last night. Either of us," Camila said.

Chase moved out of the way to give her more room to speak into the phone.

She went on. "We know you've been in a rough place for the past while and that your family is kinda shit. Since we can't be there to check on you, we're gonna bug you until you tell us what's going on."

I sat back against the couch, trying not to sigh with annoyance. "There's nothing going on. I'm good."

Chase turned the phone toward him and said, "I have to admit, you look decent. You look like you've actually slept lately."

"Yeah, I had a good sleep last night. Been eating decently too. You'd be proud." I chuckled.

There were some blurred movements as Chase set the camera down. From that angle, I could see Mo and Dylan behind them, standing around Dylan's drum kit. If I were in Toronto, I would be right there with them. As much as I missed our routine, I didn't feel the pull toward it like I might have before, even a few days ago. The desperation to be with the band at all times eased, if only mildly.

"Is this an intervention or something?" I asked as they all moved in to look at me through the camera.

"Intervention isn't the right word," Mo said, speaking louder than necessary. "We just wanted to let you know that we're all here for you. We know you've been going through it and that you don't always like to talk about it, but we're here or whatever." He waved his arms around at our friends.

"But you can, is what he's trying to say," Chase said with a lopsided smile. "You can talk to us whenever you need to."

There were a lot of reasons they had to worry about me, but I couldn't see why they would be more concerned now than the day they found out I said no to my brother's wedding. Camila had been by my place to drop off a plant of hers that was dying a few weeks ago. She'd seen the invitation on the refrigerator and asked if I wanted a date. The look on her face when I said I wasn't going made me second guess myself. Her face had twisted from concerned to disappointed.

Everyone was equally concerned when I admitted I'd changed my mind, that I decided to go. My brother and I weren't close, but I needed to be there. They knew I didn't talk to my family often. I hadn't reached out to my brother in a long time. The invitation had come as a surprise to me. Having the gut feeling that I needed to go with no rationale behind it made accepting the decision more difficult.

"I'm good, guys," I told them. "I mean it this time."

"Have you been hanging out with your family all this time?" Camila asked.

My face fell. "No. They're busy."

Chase and Camila turned their focus away from me and toward each other.

"What have you been doing?" Dylan asked as he twirled his drum sticks.

"Hanging out with friends."

Mo nodded and said, "I hope you're hanging in there, dude. We're hitting the road soon. It'll give you that boost."

"Just gotta get this wedding over and done with," I told them.

Chase reached forward and picked up the phone. Everyone else's faces disappeared until only Chase was in frame.

"So, you swear you're good?"

I nodded. I'd had a good morning, so it wasn't even a lie. "Yeah."

"Promise?" Camila asked.

"Promise."

Chase nodded and said, "Good. Now, before we get into anything to do with the new tracks, let's talk about what we're going to do with the set list for next week."

Chase set the camera on whatever stand he'd come up with. I could see the whole jam hall, everyone looking at me. It took a few seconds to get used to all of us talking while one of us was on camera, but we found our flow.

14

———

CHARLIE

After breakfast, I took the long way home, cutting through the forest and taking in the changing of the leaves. I took as many pictures as possible, as I wouldn't see as many of them once I was back in Toronto. The walk gave me a chance to clear my head. I tried not to think about Lucas, about having breakfast with Mitchell. I wanted to enjoy the crisp air and crunching leaves, but my mind refused to cooperate. My thoughts kept going back to Mitchell. Our friendship, or whatever it was, only worked because we were in Nine Pines. In Toronto, we wouldn't run into each other, we wouldn't need each other's company.

The only reason Mitchell took interest in me was because we had both become outsiders in Nine Pines. There was no doubt about that.

I broke through the tree line and stepped off the path onto our street. It was as quiet as usual, but a few of the retirees were out cleaning up their gardens or dragging their garbage bins to the curb for the next day's pickup.

"Charlotte?"

I glanced toward the voice that called my name. I recognized it, but it wasn't until I looked at the woman's face that I placed it. My mother's friend, Delia, came strolling down her driveway with a white mug in one hand while she tugged on the tea bag string with the other. She was wearing a pair of pink Crocs on her feet with little flower and bee charms.

It had been quite a few years since I had a reason to talk to Delia and I had been in no rush to do it again.

"Delia, hi," I said, straightening my shoulders and zipping up the flannel jacket I wore. I pushed some of the hair from my face and asked, "How have you been?"

Instead of stopping at the edge of her driveway, she made her way into the road and invaded my personal space.

"Oh, very good. Was that the youngest Rizzo boy I just saw you with at the Cafe?" Delia's eyes darted around as if she was holding onto something scandalous.

"Yes, it was."

Her eyebrows bobbed up and down. "I heard *that* one is trouble."

I had to be careful how I responded to the statement. The wrong words would get stories spreading around town.

"Oh yeah? Good thing we're just working on the wedding stuff together. Not too many chances for trouble."

"Be careful is all I'm saying," she told me, leaning in like she was telling me a secret. There was no one around to hear us. "You don't want to get mixed up in anything. Your parents wouldn't need that added stress."

My first thought was to question why my parents would have to know anything I was doing, but something else about the comment stuck out to me. I matched her posture. "Added stress?"

"Well, between losing his job and having to have the roof repaired this summer, I don't think your dad needs anything else."

"Losing his job?"

Delia clasped a hand over her mouth, like she was caught saying something she wasn't supposed to. If it had been anyone else, I would have been fooled by her acting. However, Delia's eyes gave her away. There was no surprise. My mother must have told Delia to keep it a secret, that Lucas and I weren't supposed to know. It was very like Delia to spill news she wasn't supposed to.

"Honey, I didn't know that they were keeping it a secret. Everyone in town knows." Delia grasped my wrist with the hand that had been covering her mouth.

I tried to pull away, but I wasn't agile enough to avoid her grip.

"Please, don't say anything to your parents. I know they're embarrassed." The corners of her mouth twitched as she spoke.

"Not a problem." I forced a smile.

The tiny, white dog of Delia's began barking in her bay window. We both turned to look at it.

"I have to go, honey. I trust that secret is safe with you?"

I nodded instead of answering. She gave a wave before shuffling up her driveway again.

Frozen to my spot. If my father was out of work, that explained the bill. It also meant that they would need me home as soon as possible.

If I hadn't been so selfish, I could have already been home. I could have been focusing on paying the bills, getting them out of debt. Maybe I could convince them to sell the house and move into a condo or somewhere they wouldn't have to worry about leaky roofs and cutting the lawn or shoveling the snow.

My dad had lost his job. I forced one foot in front of the other and made my way home.

15

———————

MITCHELL

A TEXT MESSAGE SHOULDN'T REQUIRE SO MUCH THOUGHT, I reminded myself as I strolled from the bathroom of my mom's house into my old bedroom. After tossing my towel onto the floor and slipping on a pair of boxers, I grabbed my phone from the top of my childhood dresser, which like my desk and closet door, was covered in band stickers. I grabbed a sweater from the top drawer and headed downstairs while trying to think of the right thing to send.

I almost made the mistake of writing "You up?" before realizing the connotations that went along with a text like that. The last thing I wanted to do was to make Charlie think I was texting her as an early morning booty call. Not only would Lucas give me hell if he found out about it, but I didn't want Charlie to assume I'd only shot her a message to get her into bed. However, the idea was tempting. I left my phone on the table while I went to the fridge to grab the cold brew I had made the night before. I'd assumed it would get me through a long night of pacing my mother's empty house last night, but I ended up crashing before midnight, something I hadn't done in a long time.

My phone vibrated with a text. I spun on my heel to see if

Charlie's name was on the screen, but it turned out to be Camila. I double tapped on the message until our conversation opened on the screen.

hope you're doing as good as you say you are. see you friday night.

I'd been getting similar messages from her and Chase since I arrived. They knew I was distant before leaving for Nine Pines. They knew how little I liked being back there. It was reassuring to know they were thinking about me even though I wasn't in the city. Sometimes, I needed those reminders.

Along with Chase, Camila was one of my favourite people. If anyone would be honest with me, but in the nicest possible way, it was her. Something about receiving messages from Camila, no matter what they said, was comforting.

I'm good. Can't wait to see you.

When the message was sent, I opened a conversation with Charlie. My thumbs hovered over the screen for almost a full thirty seconds before I began typing.

It's Mitchell. What is there to do in this town?

Within seconds, the message switched from 'delivered' to 'read'.

hiking?

I laughed out loud.

I am proud to say I've never actually gone on a hike.

The bubble appeared right away, letting me know she was responding.

it's just walking, mitchell. going this afternoon. wanna come?

I wanted to think of something else to offer, something that Charlie and I could do together, but everything else seemed too date-like. The idea of doing something date-like with Charlie, while not unappealing, meant there would be fallout. Fallout with Lucas, fallout with Charlie, awkwardness at Tomas' wedding. I didn't need any other reason to dread the wedding.

I'm in. Going to my gma's in a bit, so let me know when I can pick you up.

Charlie sent back a thumbs up and I smiled at my phone screen.

IT SHOULD HAVE BEEN BEAUTIFUL, BUT THERE WAS NO WAY TO focus on the changing trees and the sounds of the birds or something like that. I couldn't hear anything over the pounding of my heart. Within forty-five minutes of hitting the trail, I was panting while Charlie was up ahead, waiting on the hill for me to meet her. I stopped in the middle of the trail, bent over with my hands on my thighs.

"It's the shoes," I called out to her between laboured breaths. "I wore the wrong shoes."

"Don't blame it on your shoes." She laughed and crouched down to unzip the backpack she'd set onto the path only a few seconds before. She grabbed a metal water bottle from the bag and tossed it to me.

I caught it with one hand and took a swig from it. The water was still cool. After wiping my mouth with the back of my hand, I pointed down at my Vans. "They're not made for hiking."

"You're telling me it has nothing to do with your lifestyle? What about all the drinking and smoking weed at parties and while on tour? Is that what you do to have a good time? Punk rock and all that?"

I stood up straight. "That might be a contributing factor."

She grinned at me and I smiled back.

Charlie swung the backpack over her shoulders again and stood watching me as I struggled up the hill. I ignored my burning throat and my pounding heart to take her in. She was wearing a pair of yoga pants, fitted sweater, and a pair of burgundy hiking boots. I'd never found hiking wear appealing, but it looked good on Charlie. I especially appreciated the way her sweater rode up under her backpack, exposing how well she filled out her yoga pants.

I might have been wrong, but I thought I caught her checking me out when I pulled my sweater off fifteen minutes into the trail. Her eyes seemed to dart away when I glanced in her direction. It gave my ego a nice boost.

"Do you wanna turn back?" She asked when I made it to the top of the hill.

"Why would I want to do that?" I asked between gasps.

She smirked. "Because you're wheezing like an old man."

Since my dignity was already gone, I gave up and lowered myself to the ground. I rested against a fallen log and used my sweater to wipe sweat from my face. Charlie lowered herself next to me, bringing her backpack into her lap again. She opened the bag and pulled out a frozen gel pack.

"What's that?" I asked.

"I like my water cold," she explained as she turned toward me and put the gel pack on the back of my neck, holding it there with her hand. At first the cold was shocking, sending goosebumps all down my arms, but then I relaxed into it. Within seconds, I could feel my heartbeat coming back down to normal.

"How can a man with a body like yours be so bad at hiking?" Charlie asked.

That was flirting, right? I asked myself. Charlie Whittaker was flirting with me. I was sure of it.

"So, you noticed my body, huh?" I waggled my eyebrows at her.

She took the gel pack from my neck and dropped it on my thigh. "That's what you took away from my question?"

I winked at her. "It's okay. You don't have to pretend you weren't checking me out when I took off my sweater."

Her cheeks turned pink and she glanced into the forest around us.

I leaned my shoulder into hers. "You know, usually silence is an admission of guilt."

She shook her head and said, "I was just trying to figure out what your tattoo was."

If it had been someone else, I would have climbed to my feet, pulled up my shirt more than necessary, and let her take in every inch of my body. Women seemed to enjoy it. I assumed Charlie wouldn't be any different.

But instead, I said, "It's two robots. It's an album cover."

"Ah," she said, nodding. "The Get Up Kids, I assume?"

"Yeah, you like them?"

Her shoulders popped up toward her ears. "Hazel and Myles love them. One of their favourites."

"Speaking of loving things, why do you love this?" I asked.

"Like, the forest?"

"Hiking," I chuckled.

After a few seconds of quiet, I turned to see her staring off into the leaves of a red maple that had turned a brilliant shade of yellow. Her lips pursed and relaxed, like she was preparing them to say something heavy.

"My brother moved out of the house at seventeen. The day he finished high school, he moved into an apartment downtown with his friends and I had no one to share the household chores with. My parents were both working multiple jobs. They were never home because they couldn't afford to be." She took a sip from her water bottle before putting it back into her backpack. "When I got accepted into U of T, I started going for hikes because I needed to clear my head, to remember that I needed to go to Toronto, to university, that it was the right thing to do for the family even if it meant I would come out with a lot of debt. Out here gave me a place where I could be responsible for only myself. It's just me out here; No one else to worry about in the moment."

"You should have gone to university for yourself," I told her. "Not them."

She turned her head to look at me. Her eyelids were heavy with sadness. "My dad gave me money for textbooks my first year and when I offered to pay him back, he said not to worry about it since I'll be the one paying for his retirement home."

"Was he joking?" I asked. I really hoped he was. "It sounds like something parents just kinda say."

"He laughed. And maybe he thinks he was joking, but if I don't make enough money to care for them when they're old, what are they going to do? Who is going to take care of them?"

There was a little ember of anger in my stomach. Those were things that kids did for their parents, but Charlie was the type of person who could do so much with her life. I hated the idea of her being stuck in Nine Pines against her will, being forced into a job she hated out of obligation. She deserved more than that.

"Can I ask you something personal?" Charlie asked before I had a chance to respond to her statement.

"Sure."

"Why do you hate Nine Pines so much?"

The sun disappeared and I thought to myself how fitting it was to have gray clouds rolling in during a conversation about our lives. If Charlie hadn't opened up about her family and how it made her feel, I might not have been able to do the same.

"I haven't seen either of my parents since I got here," I told her.

"Are they busy with wedding stuff?"

I exhaled heavily. "No. This is kind of how it goes. My mom didn't tell me she was going to be in Cuba over Christmas."

"Oh."

"My dad didn't have a place for me to stay, so I ended up

having to book a room at the motel for a couple days. Even though I always came home for Christmas, I don't think he planned for me to be there."

Saying the words out loud was humiliating. Chase and Camila knew about my parents, knew how much I hated coming back to Nine Pines, but they didn't know what made it horrible. They had no idea why I turned down my brother's wedding invitation when it first arrived. I had no reason to believe anyone in my family wanted me to be there anyway.

Charlie reached out and put her hand on my wrist. "I don't know what they're thinking, but I can promise you that I'm glad you're here and it sounds like your grandma is too."

People said a lot of reassuring things to me about my family. Most of them didn't have a clue what was going on and those who did, lied to make me feel better. Charlie didn't lie. She didn't pretend like everything would be okay. She told me what she knew and that happened to be what she felt.

I shifted so I could look at her. Those big brown eyes were staring up at me. Her grip tightened on my wrist. She was giving me all the signs.

Her eyes and lips were luring me in, but I had to resist the urge. I wanted to spend time with Charlie, get to know her. If I kissed her, it would complicate those things. I didn't want to ruin my one reason for enjoying Nine Pines.

But what if I was ruining it by pushing her away?

A drop of water hit her nose, startling both of us. I forced myself to glance up at the sky, away from her. Another drop of rain hit my cheek. I wanted to curse the sky and clouds for interrupting our moment, but it realized it was for the best.

"We should go," Charlie said. As we got to our feet, the rain started coming down hard.

As she led the way along the trail, I thanked the rain for saving me from myself.

16

CHARLIE

We stood, shivering, in Mitchell's childhood bedroom. He grabbed a pair of sweatpants and a t-shirt from the drawer and tossed them on top of the dresser. I tried not to stare at his bed only two feet from where we stood. My teenage self had wondered many times what his room looked like. I didn't expect the mint-coloured walls, but the band stickers on almost every surface fit. There were posters for local bands, ones I knew my brother went to see with Mitchell back in high school. There weren't a lot of books, but I wasn't surprised to see a battered copy of Fight Club, which most of the boys read when they were young. There were stands for guitars, but no guitars in sight.

"Once you've changed, I can drive you home," he told me. He hadn't looked at me since we got back into town. I wondered if I'd misread the situation out in the forest. Between the casual teasing, the way his leg touched mine, and the general vibe between us, I assumed he wouldn't be opposed to a little making out. I knew it wasn't the best idea, but I couldn't help it. In that moment, I couldn't think of a single reason it would have been a bad idea.

It was obvious Mitchell had his reasons. I couldn't tell if it was because he wasn't interested or because he was. Neither were clear.

The whole reason I hadn't tried to flirt earlier was to keep it from being awkward when it inevitably ended, but nothing happened between us and it was awkward anyway.

He grabbed a change of clothes for himself from the drawers and shut them with his hip. He kept his eyes on the wall behind me and said, "I'll let you use my room."

I nodded and stood there, feeling ridiculous. He left, closing the door behind him.

For a few seconds, I stood there, unsure of what to do. The idea of getting undressed in his room was weird.

I wondered if I wasted anymore time, if Mitchell might come to check to see if I was snooping through his stuff. I hurried out of my soaking clothes and dried myself off with the towel he'd given me for my dripping hair. His sweat pants weren't as loose as I would have liked around my waist and hips, but I couldn't hide out in his room any longer. Once my wet clothes were folded, my bra and underwear tucked between my pants and sweater, I headed out into the hallway and toward the living room. The living room and kitchen were empty.

I was about to call out to Mitchell, but he strutted out of a room off the kitchen. He was wearing only a pair of gray sweatpants. I tightened my grip on my wet clothes, staring at his bare frame.

There were tattoos down both of his arms and across his ribs. The tanned tone of his skin wasn't just his face and neck, but carried down his torso. I tried not to stare, but my eyes refused to focus on anything other than his body. While his stomach was toned, it was his arms that made me feel unsteady on my feet. I stared at the defined muscles that flexed as he reached one arm up to rub the other. It was easy to imagine how those arms wrapped around my body. I wanted to feel his guitar-calloused hands on my hips and thighs.

He stopped at the sight of me. His brown eyes widened as they moved up and down me.

I sucked in a deep breath. I tugged at the Bikini Kill t-shirt I wore, hoping he wouldn't notice how tight it was on me compared to how it would be on him. I hoped he didn't notice my belly through the thin, white fabric or the fact the sweatpants were snug on my thighs. "Thanks for the clothes."

"They look better on you," he said as he took a few steps closer. "Did you want me to drive you home?"

He didn't look away from my eyes no matter how many times my own darted around the room. They eventually came back to him. He took another step closer and said, "Or we can hang out here for a bit."

If he hadn't offered, the courage to stay might have eluded me. I nodded at him before forcing myself to say. "Stay"

I glanced down at his bare stomach.

"I guess I should get a shirt."

"No," I said too quickly. I widened my eyes and said, "I mean, you can if you want. But why bother?"

The corners of Mitchell's mouth twitched. He patted his stomach. Nothing jiggled or rippled like my stomach would have. He kept his hand on his abs and asked, "So, are you going to stop staring at my body?"

I swallowed hard. "Only when I've figured out how that physique didn't have the stamina to make it up a slight incline."

Mitchell moved toward me until he was only an inch or two away. "I promise I have plenty of stamina."

I hugged my wet clothes to my chest. "Go-Good. That's good."

"Charlie?"

The way he said my name caused heat to spread through my entire body. I was on fire.

I swallowed hard and allowed my eyes to take in his entire physique again. Hazel had been wrong when she said I'd been with hotter men than Mitchell. She was so wrong.

"Charlie?" He said again.

I met his gaze. "Yeah?"

Mitchell's eyes moved to my lips. "You should put those clothes down so I can kiss you."

I released my grip on the clothes, letting them fall to the ground between our feet. Mitchell ran the tip of his tongue across his bottom lip. The sight of that action caused mine to part. I sucked in a deep breath as he reached out with one hand, cupping the side of my face.

"I've been waiting to kiss you since my first night back in town."

I nodded. "So, what are you waiting for?"

He stepped forward and leaned down, his lips only brushing mine at first. It was too gentle for the feeling of urgency running through me. I pushed up on my tip-toes to bring him as close to me as possible. His smile widened and I could feel it against mine. The cold that had settled in my bones from the rain disappeared at the feel of his warm mouth against mine. His tongue ran across my lips, causing my body to lean into him, desperate for support.

I placed a hand just above the waistband of his sweatpants. Goosebumps rose on his skin, like my touch stirred something in him. It was the encouragement I needed to fall against his body completely, pressing my chest flush against his. His arms wrapped around me, holding me close as our lips moved together.

After a few seconds, he pulled back, pushing strands of my still damp hair from my forehead. His eyes wandered around my face and I worried I'd done something wrong, that he might end what was happening. I wasn't ready for it to be over. I hadn't had enough of his kisses and the way his body moved beneath my hands.

"What's wrong?" I stammered out. My voice shook because of the unsteadiness of my body.

"Absolutely nothing." His eyes crinkled when he grinned.

"Good." I smiled up at him.

"That was a hell of a first kiss."

I nodded. My body ached for more. My hands threatened to squeeze him closer to me. I tried to think of a way to tell him what I wanted, what I needed, but my mind was busy trying to come up with the right words.

"You okay?" He asked, running a finger along my jaw.

"I am."

"Is this okay?"

"Definitely," I said with a short giggle.

"Good." He smiled. "I like kissing you. A lot, really."

"Me too. Kissing you, I mean. A lot."

"Can I kiss you some more?" He asked, his mouth only inches from mine.

With his lips against mine, I tried to remember all the reasons I came up with to avoid a situation exactly like that one. I knew I had a list, but none of them mattered in the moment. If there was any fall out, it would be tomorrow's problem.

EVEN THOUGH THE HOUSE WAS EMPTY, I GLANCED DOWN THE hallway before sharing the details of the night before with Hazel. I propped my phone against the fruit bowl as I lowered myself into the seat at the kitchen table. I spilled all the details of my night with Mitchell.

"So, you actually went through with it? How are you feeling about it?" Hazel asked through the phone. In the background of the video call, I could see her office, all the legal books behind her. Normally, she shared the space with three other paralegals, but they were out for lunch as a team. Hazel opted to eat at her desk so we could discuss what went down.

"It was pretty awesome. Like, he asked questions and communicated and it was different," I said between mouthfuls of cereal. It wasn't a substantial lunch, but I had too much nervous energy to stand at the stove for any amount of time.

Hazel looked up from her own lunch, pointed at me through the screen and said, "Different? What do you mean different? I thought you were just looking for some fun."

"It is. This is fun."

"Oh no."

"Oh no what?" I asked, putting my spoon into the bowl. "It was one night. It was just passing the time."

Hazel tilted her head while looking at me through the phone screen. "No, you're right back in it, aren't you? I should have known better than suggesting you sleep with your high school crush."

"He's not the guy I had a crush on in high school though. Not exactly." I knew it was a weak defense, but I believed it. When I looked at Mitchell, I didn't see Lucas' friend or the guy in high school who everyone knew would get famous one day. "He's different than before."

Hazel leaned into the camera on her phone. She got so close her pores were visible through the screen. "You're gonna get hurt."

"First of all, it was one night. Secondly, there isn't enough time to get hurt. In a few days, the wedding will come and go and we'll go back to our old lives." I sighed at the thought. "And I need to have my fun now. In a couple months I'll be moving all my shit back into this house where I will inevitably die alone. And if I'm going to give up everything to move back here, Hazel, I deserve this. I deserve to have a little fun before I really have to buckle down."

"So, this thing with Mitchell is just for fun?"

"Yes. One hundred percent, just for fun before I die alone in this town."

Hazel rolled her eyes at my dramatics. "You need to tell your parents you don't want to move back."

"Why?"

"Because I think that's a conversation you need to have with them. Let them know why you're coming home and what you're leaving behind. They assume you want to come home, that you need them. And if you want to help them, there might be a way to compromise. But you'll never know unless you talk about it."

I hated when Hazel had a point. The only thing was, I wasn't the only one keeping secrets. "Well, if I tell them, are you going to tell your parents then?"

"About what?"

"About you and how much you hate your job and how you don't want to work in law?"

"Nope." She stared off into the space above her phone.

"If I tell mine, you have to tell yours."

"This isn't the same, Charlie. Your parents want you to succeed no matter what you want to do and it's your decision to put your life aside for them. My parents have literally had my entire life mapped out since birth. My brother and sister have both followed all the plans laid out for them. I'll be disowned if I ruin the plans." Hazel kept her eyes down on her packed lunch when she spoke.

I realized I'd gone too far. She was right. They weren't the same and pushing her wouldn't make either of our situations better. In the end, I was making the choice for my parents. In her case, her parents had made choices for her. Her parents had planned every detail of her life. They had even decided what neighbourhood they would buy a condo in if they were giving her a down payment. It didn't matter that she'd been making all the payments herself. If she was honest with them, she would lose everything. Which included her car, the apartment we lived in, any money that she might have received for her parents to help her get on her feet.

"I shouldn't have said that. I know things are different for you."

"Maybe we should both be honest with our parents and when you move back in with your parents, I'll just come with you. I'll be homeless, so why not work together? If we're both living at your parents', we can pay off all your parents' debt together." She made a sound that resembled a laugh, but it was short and the sound was heavy with disappointment.

"I'll miss you when I move back to Nine Pines," I said with a sigh.

"I know. I'll miss you too." Hazel put on an exaggerated pout. There was some commotion in the background. She glanced up from her phone and then said, "Shit. Gotta go. See you Friday."

After the call ended, I sat in front of my bowl of cereal, wondering how I could make it all work. I didn't want to give up my bartending job. The room in Hazel's apartment had become my home. I really didn't want to move back to Nine Pines, but I would for my parents.

I shook the thought from my mind. I'd had a good night at Mitchell's. There was no harm in allowing myself one day to ignore the future. Instead, my thoughts turned to Mitchell's body against mine, the way we laughed at our awkwardness before we found a rhythm, before we understood what the other needed.

My face became warm at the thought and I sat back in my chair, hoping it had been as fun for Mitchell as it had been for me.

17

———————

MITCHELL

Neither Tomas nor my dad answered the phone when I called. Tomas answered a text with a simple "busy talk later." My dad didn't respond at all. I thought about messaging my mom to see if she was around for dinner, but she'd come by while I was at my grandma's. *At least*, I thought, *she left a note.*

The note on the table said she was going into Toronto for the night with one of her friends. They wanted to get an early start the next morning on dress shopping for Tomas and Gillian's wedding.

I needed a distraction to keep myself from texting Charlie. We'd talked that morning about where things stood. She was on the same page about keeping things between us casual. If we were going to do this, there needed to be some solid rules in place to keep it from blowing up in our faces. No romantic feelings. Just physical. She seemed as on board with it as I was.

We hadn't talked about the boundaries outside of what the sex was supposed to mean. Would we tell people we'd slept together? Were we both comfortable with text messages about last night? How comfortable were we supposed to be together in public? We hadn't discussed what the parameters were, which was my fault. I knew better. But her legs kept bumping mine under the table as we ate breakfast and all I could think about doing was lifting her onto the table and yanking my Bikini Kill shirt off her.

My phone vibrated and I grabbed it from the coffee table. The chat with Charlie opened when I double tapped on it.

just finished up a shift at 180. you bored?

I grinned at the screen and typed out a response to her.

Yup. Want Thai?

She responded with two thumbs up before following it up with another message.

town square in 30?

I sent my own thumbs up emojis before shoving my phone into my back pocket. I headed upstairs to run some products through my hair and mist a little cologne into the air before walking through it. Since I had nothing else to do between that moment and our meeting time, I walked downtown to meet Charlie.

When I got there, I found her on the sidewalk in front of 180 Records in the middle of the conversation with her parents. She glanced in my direction. As she listened to what her father was saying, she took small steps back as if to let them know the conversation was over. Her eyes kept flicking to me and back to her parents. I stepped in to speed up the process.

"Mr. and Mrs. Whittaker, hi," I said as I approached, pulling their attention away from Charlie. Her parents reached out and shook my hand, asking me how I was enjoying my time back in town. They paid attention to every word I said, never breaking eye contact.

"We were just saying to Charlotte that you two should join us for dinner." Mr. Whittaker nodded at me. "We asked Myles if he wanted to join us, but he said he has some work to do at the store."

"Thanks for the offer, but..." Charlie shook her head.

Mrs. Whittaker blinked at me, looking excited about the prospect of dinner. There was something about the way her eyes crinkled when she smiled that made me say, "Yes, it would be our pleasure to join you."

Charlie let out a long, exasperated sigh. "Fine."

I couldn't tell if Charlie and her mother planned it or if it just worked out that way, but Mr. Whittaker and I ended up walking behind Charlie and her mother. He put a hand on my shoulder and asked, "How are you doing? We haven't seen much of you since you moved to the city."

"I don't come back much. Been keeping busy though," I told him. Talking with parents was never my strong suit. The only ones I was totally myself around were Chase's parents.

"How's the band thing going?" He asked.

Charlie held the door open to The Cellar, one of the most upscale restaurants in Nine Pines and one of the few of that caliber who had enough patrons to stay open when the tourists were gone. While Charlie's mom asked for a table for four, I turned back to her father and explained, "Very well. Finally at a stage in my career that I don't need side hustles to pay my rent. Between tours, merch, and sales, it's enough to live on."

Mr. Whittaker clapped me on the back. "That's great. Myles was just telling us about your new record. I'll have to pick up a copy from him. Give you both my support."

It crossed my mind to laugh at his comment, to tell him not to worry about it, but Mr. Whittaker appeared so genuine. I wanted him to buy my album, and it was embarrassing to admit that to myself. I couldn't bring myself to say another word as they led us to the table near the window.

I held the chair out for Charlie and let her sit before I did. I wasn't ready to sit and engage in conversation right away. I was wondering if either of my parents knew I had a new album out. They hadn't bought the second one. I'd gifted them copies when my grandmother asked me to send her one. She paid me by sending twenty dollars in the mail. My father sent me a 'thank you' text. I never heard from my mother about it.

"Have you seen Lucas much since you've been here?" Mrs. Whittaker asked as we all took our seats.

"No, not much. He seems to be busy," I said. Before I could say much more, the waitress appeared and asked what we would all like to drink. As much as I wanted a beer, I ordered a water.

"You don't want a Manhattan?" Charlie asked from next to me. I turned to look at her. A covert smile played at the corner of her lips.

"You drink Manhattans?" Mr. Whittaker asked.

"Such a classy cocktail." Mrs. Whittaker gave a small laugh.

"And Charlie makes them the absolute best," I said, nudging her with my elbow. I hoped her parents knew what she was giving up to be with them. I wanted them to understand how grateful they should be to have a daughter like her.

Her father ordered a round of Manhattans for the table. I wondered how he could afford to bring me along for dinner. I hoped he wasn't spending the only money he had for luxuries on me. I definitely wasn't worth that.

As her parents talked about all the things they were fixing around the house, we ate pasta and salad. I realized that Charlie was so thoughtful and selfless because of her parents. They were so involved in her life. They listened to everything she said with unwavering eye contact and nods. They asked questions about school, about the midterms she would write when she returned on Monday.

"What about you, Mitchell?" Her mom asked while she cleared the sauce from her plate with a piece of her roll. Both of Charlie's parents turned their attention away from food. Their eyes locked on mine as they waited for an answer.

"Me? I'm not in school."

Mr. Whittaker chuckled. "What are your plans when you get back to the city?"

No one asked me what my plans were. My friends knew where I was going, what I wanted. I never had to justify my plans. My parents stopped asking questions about my life and goals a couple years before their divorce.

"I'm not sure," I admitted. "We, the band, have a tour and leave on Monday for that. I'm looking forward to it."

"That's very exciting." Mrs. Whittaker beamed at me. "You must love it."

I did. I loved being on the road more than anything else. It gave me the freedom to live my dream with nothing holding us back. I loved the fans, the music, and the parties. I needed to wake up in motel rooms or on the floor of some stranger's house. It's how I thrived.

I set my napkin on my empty plate. "I really do. It's the life I always wanted."

Charlie shifted in her chair and picked up her drink. The ice shook as she finished the last sips of alcohol.

Guilt coursed through my body. While I had given up everyone to live out my dream, she was giving up her dream for her family. I wondered, if I had a family like the Whittakers, if I would have given up my dreams for them, too. Some part of me said I might.

"We should go," Charlie said to her parents. "We made plans to meet up with some friends."

I wanted to interject, to tell them the truth, but it was impossible without coming off like we were hiding something.

"I'm sure they can wait a little longer," I offered, but Charlie shook her head.

I wasn't ready to leave The Whittakers. I wanted to keep talking to them about their house renovations, the plan to grow vegetables the following spring, about all the plants I kept in my apartment.

But Charlie was slipping her coat on.

"I'm just going to run to the washroom before we go," I told them. When they turned their attention on Charlie, I grabbed my wallet from my coat and headed to the waitress station. I kept out of sight as the waitress ran my card and cleared the bill.

I headed back to the table where Charlie was already standing in her coat.

"You already to go?" she asked as I reached them. Charlie turned her face toward me so her parents wouldn't see the cheeky grin she gave me. I ran a hand over my clean-shaven face.

"Sure," I said as I reached for my coat. "We can go, if that's alright with your parents."

Her parents showed no signs of getting up to leave. They were debating if they wanted to get tea or not. They glanced up at us, joining in the conversation.

"Go," Mr. Whittaker said. "You kids have fun. But not too much fun."

Charlie put a hand on my shoulder, giving me a light shove toward the door.

"I can't promise anything." She waved at her parents as we made our way between the tables to the exit.

The idea of staying at The Cellar with her parents was tempting. Instead of going back to my mother's empty house, we could discuss politics with her mother or history documentaries with her father. I enjoyed watching the way Charlie's father teased her about liking goofy comedy movies or the way her mother discussed her friends from Toronto as if she knew them like her friends from Nine Pines.

I envied Charlie. I wanted to be a part of that, even if it meant watching from the outside.

Charlie waited until we turned down a dark street before

she stopped me and said, "Thanks for being chill with all that. I know they can be a lot."

She blinked at me, thanking me with her smile and a hand on my stomach.

I cupped her jaw in my hand and said, "Nah, it was a good time. Thanks for letting me tag along."

"Come on. I'm freezing," she said, taking a hold of my wrist. "Let's get back to your mom's place and you can warm me up."

18

———————

CHARLIE

"WHERE ARE YOU GOING?" MITCHELL ASKED AS I PULLED MY sweater over my head. He tugged on the back of it before running his fingers up my back. A giggle escaped me and I allowed myself to lean back into his touch. He sat up, put his arms around my waist, and yanked me back onto the bed. My head rested on his naked stomach. The sound of his heartbeat was comforting. His arm draped over my chest and I closed my eyes.

"You want me to stay?" I asked. So much, I wanted him to say yes.

"I definitely do, but do you not want to?" Mitchell asked.

If things had been different, I might have used that conversation to lead into the "what are we" question. If our futures weren't so defined, I would have asked if he wanted to take things to the next level. Maybe we could have official dates. Maybe we could hold hands in public, kiss in public, let rumours arise.

There was also the reality that Mitchell had no plans to settle down. From what I'd gathered, monogamy wasn't on his bucket list. His life would continue in Toronto and his band would continue to become more successful until he was untouchable. I sensed it. He would forget about me as I toiled away in Nine Pines.

"Charlie?" He pushed my hair back from my forehead. His pointer finger traced over each eyebrow and then up along my hairline from temple to temple.

"Hmm?" It was hard to listen. All my focus was on his fingertips.

His touch differed from what I'd experienced with other men. He wasn't afraid to continue exploring my body. I'd been with men who wanted to cuddle and men who didn't, but there was a curiosity in the way Mitchell's hands found untouched places on my body. Mitchell was the only one who'd discovered how ticklish I was behind my knees.

"Do you want to stay?" He asked.

I rolled my head back, so I was looking up at him. "I want to stay."

His thumb traced the edge of my face. He stopped beneath my chin before lifting his thumb and brushing it over my lips. Chills spread across my entire body at his touch. I closed my eyes and listened to the sound of his heart beating beneath me.

"Are you tired?" He asked. His voice was barely above a whisper.

"No." I matched his volume.

I wondered if he'd asked me to stay because he hadn't finished with me or with my body yet. I would have been willing to stay. The awkwardness between us disappeared. We were beginning to fully understand what the other needed and liked. The sex was getting better each time.

"Wanna play Mario Kart?"

I opened my eyes. "Definitely, yes."

We climbed out of bed and headed toward the basement.

Mitchell stopped as we hit the kitchen. "Pancakes?"

At the mention of food, my stomach growled loud enough

for Mitchell to hear, as if my stomach needed to answer the question. We both laughed, and I nodded.

"You go downstairs, get warm, and I'll be down in a few minutes."

Instead of saying thank you, I popped up on my toes and kissed him on the mouth. It was so casual. Maybe too casual. He stared at me as I stepped back. There was no indication on his face where his mind went, but his pinched eyebrows and slightly parted lips let me know the gesture took him by surprise.

"I'll be downstairs," I said, backing up toward the basement door. I thought about apologizing for being too relaxed about the whole thing. Those random kisses were the type of thing I did with guys I dated, people who I saw as partners, not ones I was only sleeping with.

The only time Mitchell kissed me was leading up to or during sex. I'd been so caught up in him wanting me to stay, I read more into it than I should have.

I opened my mouth to say I was sorry, but Mitchell asked, "Chocolate chip or apples?"

"Both?" I asked with a shrug.

Mitchell took two long strides toward me and planned a light kiss on the side of my lips.

Somehow, I kept my face straight as I spun on my heel and walked toward the basement door. It was only when I put a bare foot on the wood step that I allowed myself to smile. I covered my mouth with my hand and tried to remember that in a few days it would all be over.

FOR THE THIRD ROUND IN A ROW, I DESTROYED MITCHELL IN Mario Kart. After the first time, I checked his facial expression, wondering if his mood was going to shift. One too many times I allowed myself to lose to keep the peace. When I realized Mitchell didn't care, I beat him again and again. There was no need to diminish my gaming abilities. Despite his own losses, he appeared amused by the whole thing.

"You lied," he said as he clicked on Rainbow Road. "Be honest. You don't work at The Dive as a bartender. You actually work at some retro game store, don't you? Or maybe you have your own gaming YouTube channel."

Mitchell was shirtless, sitting in only a pair of underwear on one side of the couch while I sat on the other. The two space heaters he'd turned on warmed up the place. We had discarded the blankets after a few minutes.

My loud laugh surprised me as I tugged my sweater down over my bare legs. "Remember, I have an older brother. I spent my childhood trying to beat Lucas at basically anything. I still can't beat him at Kart though."

"You got him beat in a lot of other ways now, though," Mitchell told me.

"I don't compete with him anymore," I admitted.

The day my acceptance letter came in the mail from the University of Toronto, I realized that my brother and I were on different paths. The look on Lucas' face when he saw the welcome package made me embarrassed. Not for myself, but for him.

Lucas wanting to stay in town didn't give me second hand embarrassment. That he wanted out, but had no drive to do so made me uncomfortable. Lucas was smart and he was empathetic. He only lacked the drive to get out of there.

From the corner of my eye, I noticed Mitchell glanced away from the screen as the game's countdown began. He looked at me and said, "That's really nice to hear, to be honest."

"It's just the truth." I shrugged. I didn't take my eyes from the screen which allowed me to get a head start as soon as the word GO! popped up.

Mitchell slammed his thumbs onto the controller in an attempt to catch up.

Having a significant lead, I felt confident to ask, "Why didn't you finish your psych degree? Lucas told me that's why you went to the city in the first place. It wasn't for the band, right?"

Beneath the dark shadow of new facial hair, the muscles in his jaw twitched. While I wanted to backtrack, tell him he didn't have to answer, his reaction made me more curious. I knew he had the band, but lots of people could do both.

"Honestly..." He mashed the buttons even harder. "I didn't like the things I started learning about myself." His awkward laugh didn't reassure me.

I turned my eyes away from the screen to look at him. Nothing about his tight shoulders told me his statement was amusing. His grip on the Nintendo controller left his knuckles white.

Before I could say anything, he went on, "But there was also the band. All of us were in college or university when I met up with them. At first, it was nothing serious. Just shows on the weekends at parties and cover songs in bars or for events. But when Mo joined, things just clicked. I knew then school wasn't as important. It wasn't going to take me to the places that Forever July would. We became an instant family."

I turned back to the television in time to see Toadstool drive off Rainbow Road and plummet into the abyss. "So, what was your actual reason for leaving school? The music or the family bond?"

"Huh?"

I tried to make my voice lighter. "Do you think what you love about the band is the music or the family connection you have?"

"Are you trying to analyze me?" He chuckled. "I'm the one with the half-finished psych degree."

I didn't answer right away, because I didn't know what to say. Those questions were very personal. They were the things I would only ask people like Hazel.

When I took a second to analyze my own intentions, I wondered if I just wanted to know to confirm my suspicions. The town was chatty. We all knew that Mitchell's parents were absent from their kids' lives.

After sitting with that thought for a second, I realized I wanted to make sure he had people he could call family. The ones in Nine Pines seemed to be dropping the ball, so I hoped the band was making up for it.

"I'm not trying to analyze you. I'm just making sure you're alright," I told him.

"Making sure that I love being in Forever July? Because I do."

I tapped on the joystick of the Nintendo to the left and directed Toadstool around Yoshi, passing Mitchell. "No. I just think family is important. What the family looks like isn't, but..."

"The rumours are true," Mitchell said. He tightened his grip on the game controller. "My parents don't give a shit about me."

I put my own controller down, forfeiting the race, so I could turn to him. "That's not what I said."

Mitchell set his controller down on the beat-up old coffee table and turned to me. "But that's the truth. It's fine. You're right. The band is important to me for the music, the career, but also for that connection. My two best friends, Chase and Cam. They're my family. They've got me."

I smiled and picked up the controller again. "Good."

"Aww, Charlie Whittaker cares about my wellbeing," Mitchell cooed as he reached out and squeezed my bare thigh. "You're always so worried about other people." His fingers were only on my skin for a second or two, but the warmth lasted for almost a minute after.

It was hard to ignore the protective feeling I got when I looked at Mitchell. I wanted him to be happy and safe and to know that people cared about him. Maybe, as he said, I was just worried about him like everyone else I knew. Maybe I also hoped that he wouldn't leave Nine Pines after the wedding and never come back again. When the wedding was over, we would go our separate ways, but the idea of never seeing or talking to him again didn't sit right with me.

It would, however, be better than him looking at me the way I looked at Lucas. The second-hand embarrassment that he lacked motivation to get himself out of that town. I didn't want Mitchell to come back and see me as some useless townie.

I turned my attention back to the television and said, "Pick up that controller. I want to win for the fourth time in a row."

Mitchell plucked the remote control from my hand and let it fall onto the concrete floor. He grabbed my knees and turned me so I faced him. "You already won."

I looked up into his dark eyes. "What's my prize?"

In one swift movement, he raised himself up and pulled my legs under his body. I wasn't even sure how he did it, but I had no complaints when I found myself back against the arm of the couch, the weight of his body on top of me.

19

MITCHELL

Two girls sat in a booth only a few feet away from our table. As the band gained popularity, I gained more awareness of people around me. I noticed the way men stopped in their tracks before turning toward us, like they were planning how to say something different from all the other fans. Women were more subtle and definitely shyer about their approach. They didn't seem to think they were worth my time and often hesitated or kept to themselves altogether. Spotting a fan became easy over the years.

I heard the giggles and glanced away from Lucas. The two girls were likely only fourteen or fifteen. Their eyes and mouths went wide when I gave them a brief smile and wave. When I turned back to Lucas, they erupted into laughter.

"So, I heard you had dinner with my parents last night. I thought they were taking Myles out for dinner." Lucas took a bite of his burrito. "Sorry if they were weird."

"It wasn't weird. It was a good time, actually."

"They're obsessed with being friends with our friends. That's not normal. Like, did you know Myles and his dad used to come to our house for Thanksgiving every year?"

"Your parents are cool people."

"Did they force you into sticking around for *chats* after?" Lucas said the word 'chats' in a drawn-out way, exactly as his mother spoke. He chuckled. "Is that why you didn't show up at Keith's place to watch the game last night?"

While I knew it would come up eventually, it never occurred to me to discuss with Charlie what she wanted to do, how she wanted to tell Lucas, if at all. I didn't want to make that decision for her. Either option seemed like the consequences could be negative.

What Charlie and I were up to wasn't my usual. There was a level of commitment I hadn't been expecting when it happened. We'd spent two nights together with plans to at least spend some time that evening. I enjoyed being in her company. She was down with the casual thing, with no expectations of what would happen when we both went back to Toronto. But it didn't feel as easy as it had with other women.

"Did you not get my text?" Lucas asked when I didn't answer his question.

"Your text?"

"To come to Keith's."

I cleared my throat. "Yeah. Sorry, I got distracted after I went back to my mom's place."

"Distracted?" Lucas asked, his eyebrows arching.

"Yeah."

"It's a girl, huh? That's why you ditched us?" Lucas didn't hold back his laughter. He slapped his thigh in a dramatic gesture. I sat back in the chair, hoping no one else was listening in on the conversation.

The optics were bad. I'd bailed on Lucas to hang out with his sister. It was more than hanging out. I slept with his sister while I was supposed to be hanging out with him and some guys from high school. Forgetting plans wasn't something I made a point of doing. If I made a promise, I kept it.

"Sorry, man. I don't know where my head's at." The thing was, for the first time in a while, I had been sleeping well. I'd been eating decently. I didn't wake up with a crushing feeling that life was going to end in flames.

"Who is it?" Lucas sat forward and stared at me. "Someone from town or one of Gillian's friends? Like Nina, maybe?"

I picked up my coffee and took a sip in an attempt to delay the conversation. I swallowed and allowed my shoulders to shrug, hoping it wouldn't look suspicious and would be enough of an answer for him.

"Oh, it was Zara, wasn't it? Everyone was telling me you two left together from Tyson's." Lucas' eyes darted back and forth between mine before he said, "You've never been one to hook up and tell. It's admirable, Mitchell, even if it's boring."

"I don't like to talk about women who haven't agreed to be a part of my discussions," I told him.

"I guess when you get as many women as you do, bragging about it gets old, huh?"

I didn't know what to say to a comment like that. Bragging about the women I hooked up with was trite. They weren't trophies. They allowed me to join in an intimate moment with them and I had no intention of disrespecting that. My appreciation for my friends back in Toronto increased threefold. I couldn't imagine Chase or Camila making comments like that.

"Excuse me. Hey." A young, female voice said next to us.

Lucas and I glanced up at the two teenage girls from the booth across from us. They were both holding unused napkins and one had a black Sharpie.

"I like what you've done with your shoes," I said, nodding down at her checkered Vans. "I wore the same style when I was in high school and, just like you, I wrote lyrics on the rubber too."

"They're Forever July lyrics," she said, keeping her eyes down at her feet.

"That's awesome. Thanks for supporting us," I told her

and her friend. "We love when people make their own Forever July merch. It's a big honour for us."

The girl who stood a little further back blurted out, "Can we get your autograph and a picture?"

Lucas pushed his chair back and watched as I listened to the girls talk about how much they loved the albums, that they saw Chase and I play an acoustic set when we were in town once. They asked if I had any copies of our album on hand that they could buy, but I suggested they pick up copies at 180 Records to support my favourite store in town.

After we took pictures and the girls said their goodbyes, I checked my phone to find a message from Charlie. She'd finished a short morning shift at 180 and was wondering if I had any interest in getting out into nature with her. I tucked my phone away before Lucas could get a glimpse of the screen and particularly the name on that screen.

"Booty call?" Lucas asked as I tucked my phone back into the pocket of my sweater.

"Booty call? No, I wouldn't call it that." I wondered if Lucas would talk like that if he knew it was Charlie texting me, Charlie I was spending the night with. "I should get going."

"Come by the apartment tonight if you're bored," Lucas said. "Tyson and Vic are coming by. We can get high and play poker or something."

I thought about Charlie at Tyson's, the way she got upset with her brother doing cocaine at the party. As much as I could use a night with the guys, I couldn't see myself spending another night getting high with Lucas and his friends. If Charlie found out, I could imagine her disappointment not just in her brother, but in me too.

"I might be helping out my grandma with a few things tonight." I took cash from my back pocket and put it on the table. "But when I know what's going on, I'll let you know for sure, alright?"

Once outside in the brisk air, I took the phone from my pocket and typed Charlie a message.

I'm down, but no actual hiking. Alright?

I smiled at the screen as her response came.

I guess i can make an exception for you.

20

CHARLIE

WE BOTH KNEW THE WAY TO THE SHORE, EVEN THOUGH THE PATH was no longer clear. Leaves covered the trampled ground. The locals made sure not to wear the path too thin, wanting to keep it hidden from the tourists in the summer months. It was the one piece of the beach that you could find only townies hanging out at.

Hand in hand, we broke through the tree line and onto the rocky shore of the lake. Mitchell slipped over an unsteady stone and we bumped into each other as we laughed. Once we got our footing, we stood on the small beach and looked out across the lake.

"Beautiful," I said. I let go of Mitchell's hand to get the phone from my purse. I held it up and took a picture of all the warm colours of the trees that reflected on the tranquil surface of the lake. A loon sat in the middle of the lake. It was like something out of a postcard.

"Here," Mitchell said, taking the phone from my hand. "Stand right at the water's edge."

I did as he said, putting the toe of my shoes right where the water lapped the stones. Before I could turn around to face him, Mitchell told me to hold it.

"Okay, now face me."

I eased around to face him. "Since when are you a photographer?"

"I'm not," he said, "But I wanted you to see how stunning you look today."

I glanced away, smiling.

"Look up."

I did.

When Mitchell was satisfied with the pictures, he came over to show me. I rested against him as he opened up my gallery, showing the ten different shots he took. He flipped through several. I wanted to ask if I could take a picture of him, but I didn't want to seem too forward. I didn't want him to think I needed it to show off to my friends or to tell strangers I had a *thing* with the guitarist from Forever July.

"You're a good photographer." The picture of me blushing, turning away, looked like something I would see on a curated social media account. With the water and trees in the background, it looked like an image people would use with a quote of "not all who wander are lost."

He grinned while handing my phone back. "Do you think we can get a picture of the two of us?"

I tilted my head up to look at him. "Yeah?"

With a nod, he took his own phone and held it out so we were both in the frame. He tipped his head toward me and I glanced up at him, unable to hold back my smile.

As much as I wanted to share the news with friends and even my family, that I was lucky enough to spend time with Mitchell Rizzo, the urge to keep it to myself was strong. Romantic relationships didn't come easy to me. There was always an end date. I knew what Mitchell and I had was casual, but the way he looked at me while I spoke, the way he made time for me, it was more than I'd experienced in a while. It would be hard to let go of that.

I turned back to look at the phone screen. Our faces were

awash in the golden glow from the setting sun. He took the picture.

"Can you send it to me?" I asked. "I won't post it anywhere or anything."

Posting a picture of us on social media was something that couples did, definitely not people who were only sleeping together. Even after eight months with my boyfriend, Aroon, during my freshman year in university, there were no pictures on social media. It made things easier when he dropped out of school and moved back in with his parents in St. John's. Posting pictures on social media would make things complicated when they ended. And the end with Mitchell was coming up fast.

"If you want to, I won't stop you," Mitchell told me.

I shook my head. "I'll just keep it for myself."

After he took another picture, Mitchell and I climbed onto a large rock that had been spray painted by townies. In the summer, people used it to warm themselves in the sun or sit and look at the trees and hints of cottages in the distance. Many parties had been held there in the warmer weather. Mitchell and I curled up together, arms around each other to shield us from the chilly wind coming off the lake.

"I miss this place when I'm back in Toronto," I said.

"Is that part of why you're moving back?" Mitchell asked. A gaggle of geese swooped in and landed on the shore not too far from us. We both turned to watch them.

"No. I have Myles here, but the rest of my friends aren't. I can't get a job that I really want. And..." I didn't want to say my dating options were severely limited, not to Mitchell. But it was true. Being with Mitchell during the week allowed me to forget the reality of dating in Nine Pines.

"But you have parents who love you and are happy you're around."

He was right.

"I know it doesn't replace attention or affection from your

parents, but I know for sure your grandma is happy to have you here. She was telling my mom all the things you've been doing for her." I felt a sense of pride in him when my mom told me. While my mom went on, I'd had the urge to say, "I know. Isn't he great?"

"I avoided coming back to Nine Pines because of my parents, but now I'm starting to feel guilty about not seeing my grandmother more." His chest inflated with a deep breath.

"I'm sure she's glad you decided to come for the whole week." I tilted my head up toward him. "Why did you come for a whole week?"

His eyes stayed focused on the still water ahead of us. He remained quiet for so long I wondered if he would ever answer.

"When we're not on the road, when I'm not with the band, I don't sleep that well. I get restless."

Mitchell was pretty open about his thoughts and his emotions, but even then, I sensed the conversation was heavier than either of us expected.

"Is it the city that makes you restless?" I asked.

He shook his head. "When we get back from tour, we all go our own way. I mean, I still see the boys regularly. We talk every day. Chase and I still hang out weekly, but it's not the same."

"What's not the same?" I prodded a little further. I had a sense he wanted to say it all, but wasn't sure how to.

He started rubbing some dirt from the thigh of his jeans. "The city seems empty sometimes when I'm not with the band. Then I come back here and my family…"

I leaned toward him, allowing my shoulder to press against him, to let him know I was right there. "You're lonely."

He looked at me for a second before dipping his head. "Profoundly."

It hurt to hear those words. Our agreement to be casual was hard to maintain when the overwhelming urge to hold him and comfort him tore through me. Talking openly about feelings and desires was something I only felt comfortable doing with Hazel. I was glad Mitchell trusted me enough to confide in me.

I rested my head on his shoulder and turned so I could wrap both arms around him. There was nothing I would be able to say to make his parents' neglect less painful.

"I know it doesn't make up for it, but I'm glad you have the band," I told him. "It sounds like they would do anything for you."

He kissed the side of my head and then sucked in a breath like he was about to say something else. I held still, waiting for what he wanted to say. After almost two minutes, I realized he wasn't about to say what else was on his mind. I wanted to ask, but felt like I would be pushing the boundaries of what we'd decided our relationship was.

"Did I make it weird?" Mitchell asked. "Putting it all out there?"

"No, not at all." I rested my cheek closer to his neck, taking in the scent of his cologne. "I'm glad you felt you could share that with me."

"What about you?" He asked. He rested his chin on top of my head. "What's on your mind?"

There was one thing I could share with him that I hadn't told anyone, not even Hazel because the judgment would be too much. Knowing that Mitchell would approve, it gave me relief that I could share, that I could confess.

"I should have graduated last year, but I took less classes so I could bartend more," I told him as I ran a finger over the spray-painted rock between us. I traced the curve of green paint as it merged into the blue.

"That seems reasonable."

I shook my head and pushed hair behind my right ear.

"I'm actually going into more debt by doing it this way. But I wasn't ready to give up on all the stuff I could do in Toronto that I couldn't do here. I dragged out finishing my master's degree because I didn't want to come back to Nine Pines, instead of just coming back and helping my family."

A heaviness settled on my chest. Even though I didn't fear Mitchell would judge that decision, saying it out loud was still embarrassing. I'd put my own needs and wants ahead of the best thing for my family. If I'd come home earlier, they wouldn't have bills that were three months overdue.

"You're allowed to be a little selfish."

"Is that a little selfish or a lot selfish?"

Mitchell sat back so he could stare down at me. He tipped my head toward him with a finger on my chin. When our eyes connected, he said, "You're the most selfless person I know, Charlotte Whittaker."

I got to my knees and took his face between my hands. Because I didn't know how to thank him any other way, I kissed him hard. His arms wrapped around my waist and pulled me into his lap, burying his face against me.

I tried not to picture what it would be like to spend time with Mitchell in Toronto, but I couldn't help it. It was far too easy to imagine us in bars, dancing together, or going to parties with our friends.

I stared out across the lake. The water looked deep blue as the sun disappeared behind the trees. Darkness was settling in all around us. No matter how many years passed, the sun setting early always came as a surprise.

"Wanna go back to my mom's for a bit?" He asked with his lips against my chest. "She's not home, so we can have the place to ourselves."

I nodded, but didn't say a word. We got to our feet and began our trek through the darkening woods. The cold air was causing me to shiver. Mitchell reached back and slipped his fingers between mine.

"I'm glad you're here, Charlie," Mitchell said, giving my hand a squeeze.

"Me too."

MY PARENTS' HOUSE WAS DARK WHEN MITCHELL DROPPED ME OFF that night. As it was already past midnight, there was no reason to assume either of my parents were still awake. I set my purse and keys on the entrance way table and headed into the kitchen to fill a mug full of water. A scream caught in my throat as I turned on the light to find my mother sitting at the table with her laptop open.

"What the heck?" I almost shouted at her as I clutched my chest. "You scared me. Why are you hiding in here in the dark?"

My mother pushed the top of her laptop down until it closed. She rested her arms on it, staring up at me. "I didn't hear you sneaking in." She was grinning at me, but it was a polite way of asking me to divulge what I was up to. Those smiles used to have me spilling my secrets at every turn. Once I moved away, when I got a taste for providing only the details I wanted, it was hard to stop. I got better at keeping my life to myself.

"I wasn't sneaking in." I sat in the chair at the end of the table.

"You've been staying out a lot this week."

From anyone else, it might have been an innocent comment, but it still caused a slight twinge of guilt in the pit of my stomach.

"Because I normally work at night. It doesn't make sense to change that now, and I didn't want to wake you guys up when I couldn't sleep." I shifted to hide the lie. To distract her, I nodded at her laptop and asked, "What are you doing awake at this time of night?"

"Just figuring out some financial stuff." My mom wrapped the fingers of both hands around the edge of the laptop.

"What kind of financial stuff?" I asked her.

She shook her head.

I thought about letting it go, but my mom hadn't been straight with me about their money situation for as long as I could remember. I wondered if I'd been selfish in dragging out my education to get more time at the bar. Maybe they were worse off than I thought and if I'd come home last spring, I could have helped before it went from bad to worse.

"Mom, when I move back in December, I think I should pay half the mortgage as rent," I told her. "I've been thinking about it a lot and I think that it's only fair that I do that if I'm living here."

My mother glanced down at her laptop before looking me in the eye. "Charlotte, that's not necessary."

"It's what I want to do. You and dad helped me out so much with school. Like, you paid for my books, bought me groceries, and helped me furnish the place. It's the least I could do."

My mother held up one hand to stop me. "When you finish school, you need to focus on paying off your student loans and finding yourself a good paying job."

I hated those words. *A good paying job.* I wondered if she thought my wages and tips from the bar equaled good pay. It was enough for me to live my life. Sure, things could get tough if I missed a shift. Yes, I had to let go of some little luxuries when things needed to get paid, like The Head and the Heart tickets. But I loved my job, and I loved my life. I knew my parents didn't want me to struggle like they did, but it hurt to leave that life behind. I was going to miss being behind the bar. Even making a lot of money working as a logistics manager at one of the large factories in the towns surrounding Nine Pines, I would still miss it. That much I knew for sure.

"Mom, I think—"

My mom held up her hands to interrupt me. "Let's talk about this another time. With your father. I should get to bed. I work in the morning."

I stayed still in my seat, wondering what she was doing when I walked in. I thought about checking her laptop after she went up to bed, but when my mother stood, she tucked it under one arm. She patted my head with her free hand much like she did when I was only a child.

"Make sure you get some sleep. We have a busy couple days ahead of us with wedding stuff." My mom smoothed my hair before saying goodnight and headed to bed.

The end of the week was coming up fast and for the next two days I would allow myself to pretend it could go on forever. I've allowed myself to forget that on Sunday I would be heading back to Toronto to write my last midterms, and to tell my boss I would be quitting at the end of the semester. In only a few days, Mitchell and I would be parting ways.

I reached up and touched my lips, feeling their tenderness. I would miss that feeling.

21

MITCHELL

As per Tomas' request, I drove two towns over to pick up a bunch of decorations that Charlie and the bridesmaids needed to make the bowling alley into something fit for a wedding. The trunk was filled with black fabric to hide the drop ceiling, tulle and twinkle lights for behind the wedding party's table, and boxes of realistic looking, battery powered tea lights.

I stopped downtown to get myself a coffee before heading to the venue. I needed the caffeine to get me through the rest of the day. After dropping Charlie off at home, I found it hard to settle. There were so many things we shared and I was having trouble processing how they made me feel. Trusting Charlie was easy, but I also wondered why it bothered me to share how I was feeling with her.

Making jokes about my family situation was usually how I handled such things. There were a lot of things I liked being straight up about, but my parents weren't one of them. My friends all had close family relationships with at least one of their parents. I couldn't say the same. Not even my brother called to ask me if I wanted to get food for the entire week I'd been there.

As I exited the coffee shop, wondering if Charlie pitied me or saw my estranged family as a red flag, I narrowly avoided bumping into Lucas. We danced out of each other's way. I chuckled and patted his shoulder, but he didn't smile.

"Are you sleeping with my sister?"

Lucas' words were so intense that I staggered back. I couldn't imagine Charlie telling him what we had going on between us. She mentioned she wasn't interested in everyone knowing, especially since she was moving back at Christmas. It had to be second-hand knowledge.

"Am I... what?" I said, hoping for more time to clear my thoughts, to come up with an answer that Charlie would be comfortable with.

"Did you think I wouldn't find out?" Lucas poked a finger into my chest. It hurt more than I would admit. I'd never seen Lucas as the aggressive type, but I should have known that he wouldn't be okay with how things were going between his sister and I. He'd always been protective over Charlie, even if she was doing most of the heavy lifting in the family.

"Lucas, let's take two seconds to actually have a conversation about this."

Lucas shook his head before pointing a finger at me. "A conversation about what? Isn't there some sort of code that you don't mess around with your friend's sisters? Not only did you have sex with her, but you fucking lie to me about it?"

"Listen, it's not what you think it is," I told him. I kept my hands up between us. "Your sister and I are just hanging out."

I hated saying it like that. That statement was down-playing the time Charlie and I spent together, but Lucas was the only person in town who'd treated me the same before and after I'd left. I appreciated having him on my side. When I came to town, he made me feel normal and like he wanted me there. Lucas was the only person who looked forward to seeing me when I showed up and I was destroying that.

As much as I wanted to defend myself, I needed to let him rant, get it out of his system. If I kept my mouth shut and let him get it all out, we could move on without it turning into something it didn't need to be.

"Just hanging out?" He scoffed. Lucas' pale face turned deeper shades of red as he glared at me. "Yeah, that's the problem, asshole. You don't get to use my sister and just throw her away like all the other whores you've been with."

It was impossible to stay quiet after a comment like that. Lucas could be mad at me. That didn't matter and I might even deserve it, but that comment ignited something in me. He'd turned the attack on someone who didn't ask for any of it.

"That's some bullshit, Lucas." Using the heel of my palm against his shoulder, I pushed him away from me. "Watch your fucking mouth and your bullshit double standards. You literally just praised me for sleeping around yesterday and yet you're calling women I slept with *whores*? Is that what I'm hearing?"

Lucas sneered and shoved my hand away. "You've gone soft in the city, you know that? You—"

I raised my voice to cut him off. "Or maybe you've been stuck in here for too long, hanging out with townies and doing coke on a goddamn Sunday. Maybe you need to get your head out of your ass." I took a deep breath and unclenched my fist. "You know your sister is moving back to Nine Pines and giving up everything because you can't step up and help out your parents? Do you know that your sister has a life she loves and she's giving everything up because you're only thinking about you? Maybe you need to look outside your self-involved bubble and see the world around you."

"Screw you, Mitchell, and leave my sister alone."

"No." I focused on not squeezing my cup of coffee while I

glared at him. "I like your sister. I like spending time with her and getting to know her. When this wedding is over, we're going to go our own way, but until then, I'm going to spend as much time with her as I can, because she's amazing."

Lucas opened his mouth, but no words came out.

With two steps forward, I eliminated any space between us. To my surprise, Lucas let me put a hand on his shoulder without backing away. "I appreciate your friendship, Lucas. It was never my intention to mess that up, but I like hanging out with Charlie, so I'm going to keep doing it."

I turned and walked back to my car. I set the coffee on the roof because my hands were too shaky to hold it while getting my keys at the same time.

Spending time with Charlie was one of the few good things about coming back to Nine Pines. She'd distracted me from the need to get back on the road with the band. With her, I didn't think about what was coming next, but what was happening in the present.

For the first time, I wasn't anxious to get out of Nine Pines.

"Mitchell," Lucas called to me.

I glanced at him, becoming aware of all the people watching from inside the cafe and the older couple on the sidewalk only two stores down. We had caused a scene, one that would ignite the gossip. As much as Charlie wanted to keep things between us a secret, it was too late. Lucas and I let the whole town know that Charlie and I were sleeping together.

Lucas' face lost the tightness. He shoved his hands into the front pockets of his jeans. "Just don't break her heart, okay?"

I gave Lucas a nod before grabbing my coffee and climbing inside my car. As I set the cup in the cup holder and started the engine. I drove until I was away from town square, away from any prying eyes, then I pulled over. I gripped the steering wheel hard and told myself to calm down.

22

———

CHARLIE

THE WAKE-UP CALL I RECEIVED AT SEVEN-THIRTY THAT MORNING came from Gillian begging me to pick up some self tanner, because she didn't want me looking like a ghost next to everyone else. If I hadn't spent my The Head and the Heart ticket money, I might have been able to swing the spray tan with the other bridesmaids that morning, but since I'd used almost every last cent to my name, I had to stick to drugstore tanner with money Hazel deposited into my bank account until I got paid.

It was only nine-thirty that same morning, but when I returned to find Hazel's car was in my parents' driveway. With everything going on at work, I'd assumed she would be arriving later that night or even the following morning. It was a relief to know I wouldn't have to put on the self tanner alone.

"Thank god you're here, but what are you doing here?" I asked Hazel as she climbed out of the car. "I thought you weren't coming in until tomorrow."

Hazel was still dressed in her navy pantsuit, but she had a pair of Converse All Stars on and she'd thrown her hair into a sloppy ponytail on top of her head. By the heaviness around her eyes and the slump of her shoulders, I could tell she was exhausted.

"Faked a dental emergency, so here I am," Hazel chuckled as she pushed her car door shut with her foot. "I thought with the reception tonight you might have some things you needed help with and I would rather do anything than get caught in the office at the end of the day. I would end up with more work than I could handle."

She followed me into the house, and after a brief hello to my parents, we headed upstairs to my childhood bedroom.

"Did you actually get the lightest shade of self tanner on the market?" Hazel asked as she took it out of the bag. Her eyebrows arched up above her glasses.

"I can't afford to buy a new foundation just for this wedding," I said with a sigh as I threw myself back onto my bed. I stared up at the textured ceiling. "I'm already going to have to use more bronzer than I'm comfortable with. Why did I agree to this wedding again?"

Hazel sat down next to me. "Because you're always doing things for other people, even if you don't want to."

"That was a rhetorical question," I told her as I threw an arm over my eyes. There were so many things I needed to be doing to prepare for that night, but the only thing I wanted to do was lie there.

"You doing all right?" Hazel asked.

I sat up and said, "What? Of course. I'm good."

"But?"

But the week was almost over. I would be going back to Toronto to start the beginning of the end. I would be writing my midterms for my last ever semester of university. Then, once back at work, I would have to let everyone know they needed to find my replacement before Christmas. After my finals finished, I'd begin my move back to Nine Pines.

And then there was Mitchell.

"I had everything planned. First, I would move back to

Nine Pines. I would get a job. I would take care of my family. I would eventually find someone to settle down with or, honestly, I wouldn't. As often as I thought about it, the reality of it kinda escaped me." I let out a long breath. "Now that I'm here, it's feeling really bleak. So many things will be coming to an end." I rubbed my thighs with my hands, trying to keep myself from crying.

"And?" Hazel prodded.

"I've been having fun this week, but that's only because of the parties, and you're here and..."

"And Mitchell?"

I turned to her. "I love my parents and I'm going to help them."

"I know."

"I think I just caught a glimpse of what my life could be."

"With Mitchell?"

"Well, that's the complicated part. Even if I wasn't leaving the city, it wouldn't be with Mitchell. This was never meant to be long term." I groaned. "He's focused on his band, his career, and I respect that."

Hazel gave a little sigh and put a hand over one of mine. She rested her shoulder against mine and said, "Sorry, dude. It seems like you two have really connected."

There was no arguing with that statement. We had connected. At least I thought so. For all I knew, Mitchell connected with lots of women, but for me, it was new.

I'd dated a handful of people in my lifetime, but things were easy with Mitchell. It had only been a few days, but all the awkwardness and insecurities were missing. Maybe that's how things were with Mitchell in general, not only with me.

"There's a good chance he connects with a lot of women this way." I thought speaking my concern out loud would make it less humiliating, but it didn't. His past didn't bother me, but the idea that I could be seen as one of the many in his eyes bothered me.

"Have you looked at his Instagram?" Hazel asked as she grabbed her phone from the bed and pulled up the app.

"No."

Hazel turned the phone toward me. The last picture posted on Mitchell's account was of him and I with the lake in the background. Our cheeks were squished together. My hair was blowing across my face, but I hadn't noticed at the time.

My heart began to race. It was a simple thing to do, post a picture of friends, but it felt important to me. Mitchell posting a picture of the two of us in such an intimate pose would let everyone know we had been spending time together. It made it feel real, not only something that existed within the border of Nine Pines.

"You should talk to him."

I didn't want to risk ruining our last two days together by having *the talk*. If he had no feelings outside of sex, I didn't want to find out right before walking down the aisle together. I couldn't imagine how I would fake smiles in all of Gillian's wedding pictures if it all went as terrible as I assumed it would.

"After the wedding," I said. "I think I will."

Hazel sucked in a deep breath before she said, "And I think you should talk to your parents too."

I let out a long sigh. "Not this again."

"Come on, Charlie," Hazel said.

"Do you know something I don't know?"

"No, but I realized something. You're making decisions for your parents without even talking to them about it. And I think that's a problem."

"Fine." I groaned. "But that'll have to wait until after the wedding too, because I'm too worried about what the self tanner is going to do to me."

Hazel picked up the bottle and said, "Nothing. You're going to be the colour of a ghost no matter what."

"But probably a streaky ghost."

"Most likely." Hazel picked up the bottle and said, "As long as you're not orange, I think we'll be fine."

I gave her a gentle shove. She did the same back. It reminded me that soon I wouldn't be able to walk into her room whenever homesickness grabbed hold of me. When I came back to Nine Pines, I wouldn't receive texts from her begging me to pick up Indian food from our favourite place because she was too tired from work to leave.

She was right. I needed to talk to my parents.

"Now get up," Hazel said as she got to her feet. "Let's try to apply this stuff now so if it doesn't work out, we can pumice you between venue set-up and the wedding until it looks less bad."

I got up too and grabbed the bag with other items I'd picked up at the drugstore. "Let's do this before I change my mind."

23

MITCHELL

IT WAS THE NIGHT OF THE REHEARSAL AND THE WEEK WAS coming to an end. Instead of running around and dropping things off at the bowling alley, I'd rather be in my bed with Charlie. The selfie Charlie sent me from the party room at the bowling alley made me smile as I climbed out of the car. I sent her a quick text.

At my brother's to do damage control before tonight. Parents are here. Wish me luck.

Before I could put my phone away, she wrote back.

you got this.

From the centre console, I grabbed the box holding the wedding rings. They were simple, silver bands, but I was surprised by how much they moved me. They weren't the first wedding bands I'd seen up close or even held, but something about them was different. They were my brother's wedding rings. I'd never looked at a pair before and wondered if I would ever have one on my own finger. I'd resigned myself to never getting to that point in my life.

Suddenly, I wondered if maybe I could. My fingers twitched with the need to take my phone out and text Charlie again.

"Hey," Tomas said as he stepped out onto the small porch. He pulled the door behind him and said, "Thank god you're here. Mom's been here for a total of five minutes and they've been bickering this whole time."

"Was this the best idea?" I asked with a laugh as I approached.

"I just wanted to keep everything to a minimum. I thought they could be civil long enough to make one speech together." He put a hand to his forehead. "Boy, I was wrong. The wedding is tomorrow and I have a feeling someone is going to end up in the emergency room."

"Well, I haven't seen either of them since I got here, so maybe catching up can give you a buffer or something," I told him as I handed over the wedding rings.

It took me by surprise when Tomas reached out and put a hand on my shoulder.

"Before we go in there, I just wanna say something," he said, turning to look in the front window. When he was satisfied that no one was watching us, he went on, "Things are about to get really chaotic, especially tonight and tomorrow, so I just want to say that I'm glad you're here."

The statement took me by surprise. "Yeah, no problem. Of course."

"But I wanna ask, why did you change your mind?" Tomas asked.

I glanced toward the window to check if my parents were watching as my brother had. There was no one there to witness the awkwardness in my limbs as I decided if I should put my hands in the front or back pocket of my jeans.

I cleared my throat and said, "This feels like the worst time to say this, but I honestly didn't think you wanted me here and —"

"I wouldn't have invited you if I didn't want you here."

"Well, that's nice of you to say." I didn't know if my statement came off as convincing, because I wasn't convinced by his declaration.

"You've done a lot of stuff this week, like getting the decorations, paying for a photographer, and the bowling alley. You went all out and that's more than I expected since...You know."

I nodded as I processed this information. Before, I might have brushed it off and pretended it didn't matter. But Tomas brought it up, so saying what was on my mind wouldn't be a curveball. I rubbed the back of my neck with one hand and said, "I think I projected some stuff onto you. Like, with mom and dad bailing on me for their own shit right when you went off to college out west. I'm starting to realize that wasn't really fair."

"Oh." Tomas shifted his weight from one foot to another. "That's not what I expected to hear."

"Yeah. I know."

"All you talked about was getting out of this town, so..." He shrugged.

"I mean, leaving town and cutting off my family were supposed to be two separate things." I swallowed hard, trying to push the anger back down. How did he not realize I wanted him in my life?

Tomas looked toward the windows again. "But that's what they did to us, so I guess that's what I did to you."

My anger dissipated. "And what I did to you."

Tomas laughed. "Damn, we suck as a family."

"It's definitely not our forte." I reached out and gave my brother a playful smack in the shoulder.

"Well, I'm glad you're here. I should have made that clear when I sent the invitation."

I knew things weren't instantly solved between us. There would be a lot more conversations like that one, many more awkward moments, and times when we would mess up again and again. Despite that, the conversation could be a turning point, if we let it.

"You cool with hugs?" I asked him.

Tomas chuckled. "Yeah, I'm good with that."

Grabbing my brother's shoulders, I dragged him into a hug, slapping his back a few times. When we pulled back, I said, "Well, let's get this speech figured out, shall we?"

"Please." Tomas exhaled a long, relieved sigh. "There's so much to do tonight. I can't let them ruin it."

I walked into the house with my brother. My mother was sitting on the couch with the phone to her ear. My father was standing with one hand on his hip, staring into an unpacked box filled with books. They looked relieved to see me. They moved toward me with speed, hoping to be the first to grab me and wrap their arms around me.

"Look at you," my mom cooed. "My handsome musician. Did I tell you I'm also dating a guitarist?"

"You did," I said, after placing a kiss on her cheek.

My father patted my shoulder, but he made no attempt to embrace me.

My parents' attire might have gotten more youthful, but I could see time was pulling at the edges of their faces, the corners of their eyes. They had both touched up the roots of their hair, hiding any gray before Tomas' wedding.

"Your mother always had a thing for musicians," my father said, leaning in like it was a secret, but speaking loud enough for everyone to hear. My father had been a pianist in his younger years. He also liked playing the drums. Once the divorce was finalized, he'd started helping local musicians write music. He never once offered to help me.

"I only date ones with ambition," my mother chimed in.

Tomas let out an audible sigh and excused himself to the other room.

"And I've been dating women who don't nag the ambition right out of their partner because they're jealous of their talent." My father's face contorted into an amused grin, like he'd bested her. It had been so long since I'd been in the same room with both of them. I'd allowed their hostility to fade from my mind. I wondered how long it would take until I could make that happen again.

"Jealous? I nagged you because you put yourself first and I had to take care of two kids on my own—"

I didn't stick around to hear anything else, heading in the direction Tomas left in. Through the kitchen window, I noticed him sitting on the back stoop with a joint between his fingers. I headed out to the mudroom, shoving my feet into a pair of rubber boots that were likely Gillian's by how tight they were on my toes.

"Hey," I called out to Tomas as I rounded the side of the house. "I'm gonna need some of that to get through this morning."

Tomas handed it over and said, "Promise me something, little brother. Never let Gillian and I get like that, alright? Like, if you see it happening, let me know so I can fix it, fix us, or get the hell out."

I sat down on the porch next to him and exhaled the smoke in front of me. "I won't."

I wondered if he would do the same for me.

24

CHARLIE

With the exception of Mitchell, no one seemed to notice I showed up to the rehearsal late. Everyone was going through their cues, talking about what speed to walk, discussing if they could get away with drinking that night or if they would be too rough for the wedding the next day.

"You have glitter in your hair," Mitchell whispered to me as we waited our turn to walk down the aisle toward where the minister was standing.

There had been no time to shower between completing the finishing touches on the event room at the bowling alley and the rehearsal. The other bridesmaids disappeared almost an hour before I did, leaving me to deal with all the boxes and setting up the neon sign Mitchell rented for behind the head table. One of the groomsmen stopped by to drop off the centre-pieces and ended up helping me put them on all the tables, which was the only reason I made it to the rehearsal looking half presentable.

"Where were you?" He asked.

A few eyes focused on us. By the way their bodies leaned ever so slightly toward us, I knew they were listening. Lucas wasn't the only one in town who knew about Mitchell and I. The secret was out.

I tried not to stare up at him, but to keep my eyes forward. "At the bowling alley. There was a lot left to do."

"You should have texted me. I could have come to help out."

"You were with your brother."

He snorted. "And my parents. I could have left. You would have been doing me a favour, saving me from them."

When no one was looking, I gave his arm a squeeze and turned our attention back to the minister and the woman who shouted at Amber and her partner to take long, smooth strides toward the altar. Mitchell linked arms with me like everyone paired up before and after us.

Before he began his walk toward the altar, Lucas turned around and looked between Mitchell and I. He took in our linked arms, how close we were standing, and then rolled his eyes. I wanted to apologize to Mitchell for having to deal with my brother, but it wasn't the right time.

And with things coming to an end, I wondered if there would ever be a good time.

"One more run through and we can head to The Tavern for food," Tomas called from the front of the church.

As Mitchell and I took our turn walking down the aisle toward where the minister stood, it occurred to me that one day I would be walking down that aisle too. I definitely wouldn't be walking down the aisle toward a man like Mitchell. It would be some man who had no interest in leaving Nine Pines, who didn't mind settling, whose dreams were limited to that town's limits. If I got married at all. I wondered if I would refuse to even date anyone from that town at all.

"You okay?" Mitchell asked only a few steps before we were supposed to split to either side of the minister.

"Yeah, of course," I whispered. We unhooked arms and I

moved to the side where Gillian would be standing. Once we were all in a row, we turned to see Gillian standing with a bottle of champagne in place of a bouquet. She walked her way down the aisle, laughing and winking.

I glanced over to where Mitchell stood. At first I thought he was looking in my direction, but then I noticed his eyes were on his brother. He looked between Tomas and Gillian before turning his focus to the ground. It occurred to me he'd asked if I was okay because he needed me to ask him if he was. I'd let him down.

Standing still became a chore as the minister ran through the process and told them to remember their vows. I tried to catch Mitchell's eye, but his attention was on his own hands. My cousin, Amber, turned to me and said, "What's with you tonight?"

"What?"

"You're jumpy," she hissed.

"Sorry. I'm hungry," I lied. It was the easiest answer. If everyone knew about Mitchell and I, there was no reason to fan the gossip flames.

I leaned to look at Mitchell again, but it was Lucas' eyes I caught. He shook his head in disappointment. The muscles in his jaw tightened when he stole a glance at Mitchell.

"And now, Nina, you can hand the bouquet back to the bride," the minister said. Nina handed the champagne bottle to the bride. Gillian didn't wait to pop the top off. A little plume of gas escaped to the cheer of almost the entire wedding party.

The only people not smiling were Mitchell, Lucas, and I.

"To the Tavern," Tomas said, pumping a fist in the air. "Dinner is on us."

As everyone headed toward the exit, I hung back, hoping that Mitchell would do the same. A breath of relief escaped me when he did.

"Are you okay?" I asked him, keeping my voice down. We

began following the rest of the wedding party, but our pace allowed us to lag, giving us space to talk without being overheard.

"Of course," he said. It was almost the exact words I'd used in response to him. And like mine, they didn't seem genuine.

"You sure?"

"I am," he said. He pulled the phone from his back pocket. It was buzzing in his grip. The name "Mo" showed up on the screen. My Forever July knowledge was slim, but I knew Mohammed was their bassist.

"I have to take this," he said.

"I'll meet you outside then?" I asked.

He nodded before swiping to answer the call. Even though I picked up speed as I headed toward the door, my feet were heavy with hesitation. I wanted him to tell me it was okay to stick around, that the conversation would only take a minute, but when I glanced back, his back was turned to me.

When I thought about the next day or so, I thought about how it would be nice to spend it with Mitchell before everything came to an end. I'd been hoping to get it all out of my system, giving it everything in our remaining hours. It was clear to me Mitchell wasn't feeling the same way.

I stepped through the double doors to find it raining. Everyone was huddled under the awning, passing the champagne bottle back and forth. As soon as they saw me, Lucas pushed the bottle into my hand and asked, "Where's your boyfriend?"

"What?" I asked, trying to play it cool. The wrong answer would confirm the rumours, but also give them something else to spread around. If they knew we were sleeping together, that was one thing, but I didn't want people putting heavier expectations onto the two of us. I didn't want to be yet another reason Mitchell refused to come back to Nine Pines.

"Yeah, what's up with you and Mitchell?" Gillian asked.

Amber, Nina, and Gillian all exchanged glances between each other. Even the men listened in, wanting to hear what was going on.

"Nothing," I told them. "We're just friends."

"Friends who are going to hang out when you're back in Toronto?" Amber wiggled her eyebrows up and down at me. In the light hanging above the church door, I saw all of their faces watching me, waiting for me to give them the gossip. I allowed my eyes to look past them all to the glistening pavement of the parking lot.

The door opened, bumping into Lucas and I. Everyone adjusted to make room under the awning, shoving me against Mitchell. He put a hand on my lower back to keep me steady. His hand didn't linger as long as I wished it would.

"Sorry to do this, but I gotta head out," Mitchell said to everyone. He turned to Tomas and Gillian. "Your photographer is waiting to be let into mom's house."

"Are you going to come by after?" Amber asked him. She winked at me.

"We'll have to see." Mitchell gave them a reassuring smile, but anyone could tell he wouldn't be meeting us later. The tightness in his shoulders spoke the truth.

"Who's coming with me?" Tomas asked, holding up his keys. Amber shouted that she would. Everyone left the church steps, heading toward the cars. Only Mitchell, Lucas, and I were left standing there.

"Do you want a drive?" Mitchell asked me. "I can drop you off on my way home."

Every bit of me begged for my mouth to say yes. I wanted to spend that extra three minutes alone with him. I even wondered if I could stall and get a chance to make out in the back seat before he went home. But I shook my head. "I think I'll get a ride with Lucas. You've gotta go."

Mitchell turned to face Lucas, who was still standing under the awning, waiting to see what transpired. Mitchell shoved his hands into his pockets and said, "I would come if I could. It's just—"

"I know. Your friends are here." I said to Mitchell.

He nodded.

A sense of hurt filled me when he didn't invite me to come along, but it wouldn't make sense to introduce his friends to a girl who they would never see again. It would be unnecessary and a waste of an awkward introduction. We weren't a couple.

"Go, see your friends. We're going to pick up Hazel and Myles on the way anyway," I told him.

It surprised me when Mitchell leaned forward and planted a soft kiss on my lips. He did it right in front of my brother. People could see from their cars. He brushed a strand of hair from my face and said, "I guess I'll see you tomorrow."

"I'll see you tomorrow." My words were barely audible over the starting of Tomas' car. Mitchell clapped Lucas on the shoulder before rushing out into the rain toward his own car. I watched him go, a little annoyed at myself for being disappointed.

I was certain there was a connection between us that was deeper than meaningless sex. At least, there was for me. Mitchell might have made a lot of girls feel that way. Even if he didn't, even if things between us were different, it was pointless.

What we had was doomed from the start. That was what made it work. There was an end date that was always at the back of our minds. We were supposed to go our separate ways without getting hurt, without complicating things. We had our own plans, our own lives to live. He would not give up his band and I wouldn't give up my family.

"I told him if he hurts you..." Lucas cleared his throat. "You just give me the word."

"This thing was always going to end like this," I told my brother. "No one's going to get hurt, because there's nothing to get hurt over."

Lucas took that answer at face value and said, "Well, let's get to The Tavern, alright?"

It was impressive how easily he accepted the lie.

25

MITCHELL

THERE WERE ONLY A FEW TIMES MY TORONTO FRIENDS HAD visited Nine Pines and of those times, they'd never come to my mother's house. I became aware of things that they might notice, things I hadn't thought about in a long time. One of those things was how my mother had replaced all of our family pictures with her own amateur paintings. Camila wouldn't say anything about how terrible the paintings were unprompted, but I could see it in the way she nodded her head and pressed her lips together.

"What do you think?" I asked her, wondering if she would crack. I tossed an arm around her shoulder and said, "Do you think they're worth giving up your career for?"

Camila turned to look up at me, pushing her dark curls away to make sure she made eye contact. "Her passion is admirable."

If anyone knew art, it was Camila. Not only was she a celebrated photographer, but Camila also was the co-founder of a publication that focused on art in many mediums. She had an eye for finding people with hidden talent, people who didn't know how good they were. She could see the good in so many people. It was one of her biggest strengths.

I laughed and said, "She has a passion for it, that's true. She gave up almost everything for her art."

"Hmm." Camila wrapped an arm around my waist and said, "Kinda like you and the band."

"Um, no." I twisted my torso so I could let her see my disappointed scowl.

What my parents did wasn't the same as what I was doing. My parents had big dreams, and they allowed themselves to get so caught up in each other they forgot about them. I would do everything in my power not to hurt people that way. If I stayed focused on the band, no one would get hurt.

She gave my side two pats before breaking away and heading into the kitchen where Mo was microwaving some leftovers they picked up before getting there.

"It's a cute town, but everyone knows we're here for the wedding," Mo said as he popped open the microwave door. He stuck his finger into the belly of his burger before pulling it out.

Mo loved small towns. Having grown up in Toronto, he didn't get exposure to the small town experience until Forever July began touring more often. Much like myself, as soon as we returned to Toronto, he was making excuses to leave again. He'd been vacationing in small towns ever since. He liked the quiet. Mo would thrive in a place like Nine Pines. I wouldn't.

"Wait until you get to the wedding tomorrow. Everyone's going to treat you like you're old friends," I said with a laugh. I pulled open the fridge and grabbed two beers, handing one to Camila. Turning to Mo, I said, "I have beer, coke, sprite, or pomegranate juice."

"Pom juice," he said with his mouthful.

I handed him a bottle.

"You look really rested," Camila said as the three of us headed into the living room. "You don't look so..."

"Haunting?" Mo offered.

"I was going to say *haunted*." Camila shrugged.

We laughed, because it was true. Sleeping for eight hours a night and eating more than one meal a day had improved me in more ways than I'd realized at first. Getting out in the fresh air with Charlie might have contributed to that as well.

"Cooking for my grandma has made it easier to eat three times a day," I told them. "I'm glad you guys are gonna get to see her tomorrow. She's been asking about you."

"And the girl you've been spending your time with?" Mo waggled his eyebrows at me before brushing a piece of French fry out of his short beard.

"Who said there's someone I'm spending time with?" I asked, raising an eyebrow.

"You haven't sent a single complete riff since you got here." Mo laughed.

The words settled onto my chest. I sat back in my chair and pulled at the corner of the bottle's label. Mo was right. I hadn't focused on my music at all since I started hanging out with Charlie. Sure, it was only a couple days, but never had I gone so long without my music. I'd been distracted by time spent with Charlie. I'd allowed myself to get caught up in the simplicity between us.

Mo swallowed down some food and said, "Also, the Instagram post. You never post girls on social media."

"I post Cam and Peyton on my Socials all the time."

Mo tilted his head to the side and said, "Not the same."

"You're allowed to take a break," Camila said.

I glanced up at her, finding what I could only guess was a look of concern. Her eyebrows pinched and her lips pressed into a fine line.

"It's just a break," I told them. "This is just a little vacation from real life or whatever. That was the point of all of this, right?"

"The point of coming to this wedding?" Mo asked, no

longer joking. He set the take-out box on top of the table place mats. "For some reason, I thought you were coming here to connect with your parents or whatever. Hash things out."

Camila cleared her throat and shot Mo a wide-eyed look. Mo's shoulders pulled up to his ears in defense.

"I never said that," I told them.

"I know," Camila said. "Chase, Mo, and I were hoping that's what you were doing here."

"Sorry," Mo mumbled.

I ran my empty hand through my hair before taking a mouthful of my beer. I swallowed and said, "Even if I wanted to, they're too busy. Not too busy to be at each other's throats though."

Because sitting there was humiliating, I got up and went into the kitchen. I slammed my beer down on the counter and reached for my phone without thinking. It was only when I opened the messages that I realized I wanted to talk to Charlie.

Messaging her would be a bad idea. I couldn't use someone I'd only really known for a couple days as a crutch when things were getting rocky. I needed to deal with it on my own, because after tomorrow I wouldn't have Charlie to reach out to. She would finish her exams before coming back to Nine Pines. I would end up distracted by her, ignoring the band, forfeiting everything I worked for.

"We're sorry we brought that up," Mo said from behind me. "We thought it was something you wanted to share, something big."

I shoved the phone back into my pocket and turned to face them.

Camila gave me a sympathetic smile. "We love you, Mitch. We wanna make sure you're good."

"It's true." Mo nodded.

"My brother and I had a talk. It was awkward, but it was

something," I told them. "We realized we were avoiding each other for all the same reasons: our parents."

Camila nodded.

"So, we talked about making plans to see each other once a month when I'm not on the road. I come here one month and he comes down with my grandma the other month."

Once a month didn't feel like a lot, but it would be a start. My brother and I needed to get to know each other better. We needed a chance to make sure we could stand seeing each other that often. The connection to my family was broken, but I wanted to try to fix it.

"That's awesome," Mo said.

"That'll be good for you." Camila smiled. "I can't wait to hang with your grandma at the wedding tomorrow."

"Don't forget you need to be taking pictures of everyone tomorrow, not just Gigi Rizzo," Mo reminded her.

The idea of Camila focusing on my grandmother during the wedding and reception wasn't a stretch. Camila had a way of finding the beauty in people who may not be considered attractive in the eyes of society. It was one thing I appreciated about her.

I was grateful that I would be seeing my grandma and Tomas more often. I was glad that my brother and I had a chance to discuss how things had been between us. If only I could get my parents on board with the reconciliation.

"Thanks for being here, both of you," I said as I picked up my beer again. "I love you guys."

"If you love us so much, you'd tell us about the lady you were posting on Instagram." Mo arched his eyebrows at me. Camila tilted her head to let me know she, too, was waiting to hear about Charlie.

I wrapped my arms around the necks of both of my friends and led them back to the living room.

26

CHARLIE

My mouth tasted like beer when I whipped the covers off myself. I swung my legs off the side of the bed and touched something on the floor. I tucked my feet back up before glancing over the side to see what I'd touched.

I'd forgotten Lucas passed out on the floor when we got back from the bar. He had every intention of going back to his old bedroom, but he stayed because I was both drunk and sad. I made him listen to how I'd developed feelings for Mitchell and how it was embarrassing because we both said it would be casual. Lucas didn't even react when I told him I'd had my fair share of one-night stands and casual sex, but that this was different, despite the rules. We had rules, and I'd messed up.

"Hey," I said as I prodded his side with one of my big toes. "Get up. It's the big day. It's the wedding day."

There were already voices downstairs. I picked up my phone to check. It was only seven-thirty. My alarm wouldn't go off for another forty minutes. Out the window, the sky was heavy with rain clouds. I hoped the photographer had back-up locations for indoor pictures. I was too tired to worry about where a good spot to shoot would be.

"You feeling better?" Lucas asked while pulling himself up onto my bed. He crawled past me and collapsed against my pillow.

"Yeah. Thanks for listening to me. I think the alcohol enhanced my emotions," I told him. I flopped back onto the bed next to him. "I think I'll stay sober tonight."

"I might too," Lucas said.

I turned my head to look at him and raised my eyebrows at him.

"What? What's that look for?"

"You haven't really been sober since I got here." I bit my lip while waiting for his reaction. It wasn't my intention to bring it up before the wedding, but I couldn't pass up the opening.

Lucas covered his face with both hands. "I assume this is why Mitchell called me out."

"What?" I propped myself up on one elbow to look down at him. "Mitchell said something to you?"

Lucas avoided looking at me. "He let me know why you're coming back to town in December."

There was a loud burst of laughter from downstairs. We both went quiet, waiting until the sound eased again.

"What did he tell you?" I asked.

"He told me that you're coming back to help mom and dad because they aren't doing well with money. Then he told me I need to get my shit together 'cause I'm ruining your life by being a low-life or something." Lucas sat up and tried to tame his hair. It was greasy and stuck up in multiple directions.

I raised an eyebrow.

"But he didn't say it like that."

I bit my cheek to keep from smiling. It never occurred to me that Mitchell would swoop in to try to fix things. At the same time, I worried about Lucas' feelings about being called out.

"I wasn't trying to…" I cleared my throat. "I was just upset about having to move home. It's my choice to help them."

Lucas twisted to look at me. "I wanna help, Char. I gotta get out of this rut first."

I sat up too, so we could be on the same level. After bumping his elbow with mine, I asked, "When I'm back, I can help."

He patted my knee. "Nice of you, but I think I need to get out of this town. It's come to my attention that my lack of worldly knowledge is making me an ass."

I let out a small sigh.

"Where do you wanna go?" I asked him.

He shook his head and shrugged.

"Why don't you come to Toronto? I can help you look for a room somewhere. If you like it, Hazel will need a roommate in December."

Lucas picked at the skin around his thumb for several seconds. He glanced up and said, "I have to think about that. It would be nice to know you, Hazel, and Mitchell over moving somewhere I'd know no one."

There was one thing I needed to say and holding the words back made my throat burn. If I said it out loud, there would be no more taking it back. We would have to face what was going on.

"There are plenty of drugs in Toronto too, Lucas," I reminded him. I swallowed hard.

Lucas got up off the bed and began pacing in the small space in front of it. He picked up the make-up mirror I used and stared at his reflection. He blinked at the image of his face and then looked at me.

"I have to try." His voice came out in a whisper. "I need to get away from certain people and start fresh."

"You'll have to come back some day," I reminded him. "Our family is here."

"It sounds like you don't want me to do this."

"I do. I just want you know to it's gonna be hard."

He tipped his head down. "Don't you think I know that? I need to do something, Char. I need to try, right?"

I got up off the bed, put my hands on Lucas' shoulders, and said, "That's what I like to hear."

While we'd grown up pretty close, Lucas and I weren't the type of siblings to hug.

But the moment called for it. I tossed my arms around his neck. At first, he stood rigid in the embrace before squeezing me back.

"Thanks," he said. "I think I needed that."

Before I could respond to him, someone knocked on the door. There was no time to answer before our mother pushed the door open. Her eyebrows pinched together as she looked at us.

"Everything okay in here?" she asked.

I forced my lips into a smile. "Yup. Just trying to get motivated to go downstairs into that madness."

"Motivated or not, you have to get down there." My mother chuckled. She opened the bedroom door all the way, allowing the voices from the living room to carry in. Lucas and I winced at the same time, then laughed together.

"Let's do this," Lucas said, wrapping an arm around my shoulders and leading me toward the hallway. Our mother laughed and followed us into the wedding madness.

THERE WAS NO TIME TO THINK ABOUT MITCHELL OR TORONTO OR quitting my job. The wedding chaos was in full swing. There were bridesmaids drinking mimosas while the stylists and make-up artists wrangled everyone into chairs. The photographer wandered between it all, dodging elbows and champagne flutes to get some of the best pictures. By the time hair and make-up finished, we all looked like models out of a bridal magazine.

The awkwardness with Mitchell from the night before crept back in as all the pieces of the day fell into place. I didn't have to run around for Gillian anymore. She had something borrowed or something blue. There was no reason left to call the bowling alley to check on the status of things. There was no running to the store to pick up orange juice with pulp because the maid of honour thought pulp-free orange juice was pointless. By the time we were supposed to be ready, when it was almost time for the ceremony to start, I was exhausted. The day was just beginning, and I was certain I would fall asleep before dinner was served.

The sounds of voices and music in the church let me know it was almost time. I stood in front of the room's full-length mirror and stared at the black fabric of the dress. I smoothed it down for the tenth time and made sure not a single hair on my head was out of place, not a smudge of mascara was visible. I glanced back at Gillian, wondering how she could be so calm before walking down the aisle to the man she would be with forever.

"In less than thirty minutes, you're going to be married," Nina said before taking one last sip of the pulpy, champagne-heavy mimosa.

Gillian stood from the seat she's taken by the window. The light caught the sequins on the bodice of her flowing dress. Everything about her looked flawless. She touched her bare collar bone and said, "I never thought Tomas would settle down, but this was all his idea."

"You locked that down."

Everyone laughed, talking about how Tomas used to party a lot and sleep around.

"Charlotte, we thought you might be on your way to locking the other brother down," Nina said. There was no amusement in her tone. It wasn't a joke, but everyone else seemed to think it was. Her eyes bore into me as I occupied myself by refilling my mimosa.

My stomach twisted with nervous energy and my hands shook. "I'm not trying to *lock* anyone down."

"Well, I am," Gillian said, turning the conversation back to her, where it rightfully belonged. The room erupted into laughter again.

There was a knock on the door and my uncle, Ron, peeked his head in. He looked at Gillian and said, "Sweetheart, are you ready?"

After a period of calm, things became frenzied. Everyone made last checks on their hair, make-up, and dresses. I slipped my feet back into my black pumps. I tried to focus on Gillian, about remembering to be cautious with my steps, to not rush down the aisle, but all I could think about was seeing Mitchell.

I was worried he would be awkward. Now it was over and we were giving up on pretending that life could always be easy and fun. I feared the wrong thing would slip out and he'd know how much I'd miss him. He wasn't even gone, and I already did.

The bridesmaids were ushered into the hallway where we'd meet and link arms with the groomsmen before walking down the aisle. I was glad to be handed a bouquet of white roses to keep my hands steady.

The hallways were narrow and as we lined up, I tried to catch a glimpse of Mitchell. I wasn't able to see much more than the top of his head and his shoulders. With only a moment of eye contact, I could prepare myself for what might come next before we were standing in front of all the wedding guests, before we linked arms and began our march toward the altar.

The music changed from soft hymns to the sound of an Ed

Sheeran song. I glanced back to look at Gillian. Despite how frantic she had been all week, I saw a calm in her. She knew it was the right thing, and she was ready for it to happen.

One by one, the bridesmaids headed down the aisle. As each of them stepped forward, linking arms with a groomsman, Mitchell came into view. Then we were standing in front of each other. As instructed, we moved toward, keeping our eyes on each other. We stopped in front of the door, giving pause. He took a deep breath and smiled at me.

"You look amazing," he whispered.

I wished we were anywhere else, so I could take his freshly shaven face in my hands and press my lips to his. His hair was pushed back off his face. His suit was fitted and showed off his strong arms.

"So do you." I grinned up at him.

He turned and offered me his arm. We turned to face the church filled with people. I'd allowed myself to forget the audience we had. At least, I reminded myself, everyone's attention would be on the bride. No one would notice the way I couldn't stop grinning.

We made our way to the altar and Mitchell let go of my arm, allowing me to walk in front of him to where the bridesmaids were standing. I wanted to stare at him the entire time, but the music changed to Pachelbel's Canon in D. Everyone rose to their feet. Every head turned to see Ron escorting Gillian down the aisle.

Despite seeing her in the dress already, I couldn't help but be blown away by her and her entrance. She came down the aisle with a huge smile. Her eyes softened as she focused on Tomas, the love of her life.

Of all the people out there, of all the men that passed her by, she'd found someone who was enough, someone she could really fall in love with. They'd lived in the same town for most of their lives without ever crossing paths. They left for school and when they came back, it turned out to be the perfect time. So many things had to align for that to happen.

I glanced over at Mitchell. As if he could feel my attention, he turned to look at me.

Mitchell and I would never have a story like Gillian and Tomas'. We were doomed from the start.

27

———————

MITCHELL

BY THE TIME WE FINISHED ALL THE PICTURES, MY CHEEKS HURT from holding a smile. It was especially hard to do when Tomas and I were sandwiched between our parents. If the photographers had been anyone other than Camila and Mo, I never would have been able to fake it. It was Mo making bunny ears behind Camila that got me through everything with a couple of laughs.

I was waiting for all the picture taking to end, so I could talk to Charlie. She deserved an apology for the weirdness from the night before. I should have invited her to the house. There was no harm in introducing her to Camila and Mo. They had met plenty of women I'd slept with over the years. Some of them were even friends with them.

"You're being weird," Camila said as we headed to her car.

The rest of the wedding party headed to the bowling alley while we finished up the family photographs. Both of my parents offered me a drive with the obvious condition that I listen to them rant about the other. The intention had always been to ride with Cam and Mo to the reception.

"I'm not being weird."

Mo let out a snort of laughter.

Camila rolled her eyes. "Dude, one minute you're making heart eyes at the girl and the next minute you're standing like a statue next to her for pictures, afraid to touch her."

I climbed into the back seat and loosened my tie. It was suffocating.

"It was hard to watch," Mo chimed in.

"We're just in an awkward phase in our..." What was the word? Relationship would imply something other than what it was. Fling sounded too casual and too archaic. "Things are almost over between us, and I'm not sure how to act."

"Strange," Camila said. She dragged out the 'a' in the word, letting me know she was suspicious of my statement. She turned on the car and began backing out of the parking spot. "Because when you and I were hooking up, you weren't acting suspicious after deciding it was ending."

In front of Mo and I, she could use our brief dalliance against me. In most settings, Camila avoided talking about when we'd slept together. She was embarrassed because the only reason she started hooking up with me was an attempt to get over her unrequited crush on a woman she'd worked with at Henry's Cameras. But our friendship was important to us and we didn't want anyone to assume we'd ever be more than friends. Neither of us wanted that.

"Because you and I decided it was ending," I reminded her. "Clear boundaries were always set with us. We were always on the same page."

Mo turned in his seat. "And there were no boundaries with Charlotte?"

"Charlie," I corrected him.

"And you didn't set boundaries with *Charlie*? You're not on the same page?"

"We had boundaries," I told them.

I rested my head against the back of the seat. I didn't know how to answer that. We both agreed to a brief affair. We both had our lives going in different directions. I had goals to hit. Forever July was my life and being back with my friends reminded me of that. I'd been missing them, my true family, and I couldn't let my feelings over a woman get in the way of that.

I wasn't sure we were on the same page.

"You're falling for her, aren't you?" Mo asked. He reached back and patted my knee. "I get it. She's really cute."

"I second that," Camila laughed. "She is super cute."

I let out a long sigh. "Yeah. She's pretty awesome."

THE BOWLING ALLEY RECEPTION TURNED OUT BETTER THAN I'D expected. The event room had transformed into a magical place. I hadn't been around for the finishing details, but the fabric on the walls and the lights behind the main table all added a soft ambience in direct contrast to what was happening outside the doors. There were fairy lights on every table, giving everyone's face a warm glow. Charlie and the bridesmaids had thought of everything.

Throughout dinner and speeches, I forced myself not to look at the table at all, worried my focus wouldn't remain on the bride and groom. I listened to those who spoke. I ate my meal and allowed one of the other groomsmen to bring me beer after beer. When the plates were cleared from the table, when the music changed to something more upbeat, everyone started getting up from their tables. It was the right time, I decided, to talk to Charlie and clear the air.

Before I could get out of my chair, Tomas came over and patted me on the back.

"Thanks again for being here, bro. The venue and the photographer... I wanna pay you back." Tomas looked dead serious.

I shook my head. "Nah, they're wedding presents and to

make up for all the times I didn't come home for birthdays or Thanksgiving or —"

"Yeah, I get it," Tomas said with a loud laugh. "Well, when you get married, I'll return the favour."

I glanced toward Charlie's chair. It was empty.

"Who are you looking for? The photographer?" Tomas patted me hard on the back. "She's hot. You should go for it."

"Cam? No, we're friends. Do you know where Charlie went?"

"Charlotte Whittaker?" Tomas asked.

"Yeah."

We both scanned the room, but there was no sign of her. I realized the table where her friends, Hazel and Myles, had been sitting was also empty.

"Maybe she's outside with her burn out brother. They're probably getting high." Tomas kept his voice low, but not his chuckle. I wanted to ask why Lucas was in the wedding party if Tomas had such a problem with him, but I realized it was likely because of Gillian as she floated over to us.

"What's wrong?" Gillian asked. She planted a kiss on Tomas' cheek before turning back to me with a questioning look.

"He's looking for the Whittaker siblings."

"Oh, I sent them to go pick up some limes. The ones this place has aren't great, like, at all." Gillian shrugged before waving at someone in the distance and disappearing toward the dance floor.

Of all the people in the wedding party, she had to ask the one person who had gone above and beyond already that week. It occurred to me to say something about it, but it was the wrong time. It was their day and I couldn't let my mood get the better of me.

"Wanna come bowl a game with me?" Tomas asked.

I grabbed my beer from the table, threw an arm around my brother's neck and said, "Yes. Let's do it."

28

CHARLIE

EVEN THOUGH LUCAS WAS SOBER ENOUGH TO DRIVE US, WE decided to walk and enjoy the warm October evening. The air was misty and my hair was falling out of its curls, but it didn't matter anymore. The pictures had been taken. Everyone was getting too drunk to notice. In a couple of hours, the night would end and it wouldn't matter how nice my hair looked or how dewy my skin had become.

Myles and Hazel were ahead of Lucas and I as we reached the Nine Pins parking lot. I swung the bag of limes back and forth as we made our way toward the door. When Myles and Hazel stepped inside, Lucas grabbed my arm and said, "One sec."

"What's up?" I asked, facing him. I tightened my grip on the bag of limes, worried he would tell me he'd used drugs again or that he'd rethought leaving Nine Pines. My eyes went wide as I waited.

"Are you and Mitchell being weird because of me?"

I laughed. "What?"

"Because I yelled at him for sleeping with you?" Lucas went to run his hands through his hair and remembered he'd styled it for the wedding. He adjusted his suit jacket instead.

"I shouldn't have said anything, but I was worried and now you two barely look at each other."

I put a hand on his shoulder. "It's not you. It's just weird."

"Did something happen?"

The answer could be simple, so I started with that. "I'm going to miss him and I didn't think I would."

The truth was much more complex than that. I would miss him, yes, but I would miss the connection we'd developed in the last few days. Mitchell had gone from a stranger to a friend in a matter of one conversation. I hadn't noticed right away, but looking back, it was clear. My feelings developed for Mitchell so fast and just as quick as it started, it was all ending.

Lucas shifted his weight. "I didn't like the idea of you two together at first. But now it kind of makes sense to me."

I laughed. "It does?"

"You two could be good for each other. You're both so single-minded and it would take a lot of compromise for it to work, but it would make you both better people."

Lucas often played the role of older brother, but his statement made me appreciate it so much more than before. I patted the side of his face. "Thanks for being a good big brother."

"Thanks for being an awesome little sister." He nodded his head toward the door. We both looked to find Mitchell standing there. I raised my hand and gave him a small wave. Lucas took the grocery bag from my hand and said, "I'll see you two inside." As he walked past Mitchell, he gave him a nod.

"I thought you'd left," Mitchell said as I approached. At some point, he'd run his hands through his hair, messing up the slicked back look he'd had earlier. His tie was missing and the top button of his shirt was open, exposing a hint of his tattoos. He looked more like himself now than he had earlier in the day.

"I wouldn't leave without saying goodbye," I told him. "I just went to pick up some stuff for Gillian."

He reached out and put his hands under my coat, resting them on my waist. I stepped forward until there was no space between us. It should have been comforting, but I could tell what was coming. The air might have been warm for October, but I shivered.

"I know you like doing stuff for people, Charlie, but don't sacrifice everything for other people, alright?" He leaned forward and planted a light kiss on my forehead.

I closed my eyes. "I'll try."

"I wanna apologize for being weird last night. I should have invited you to meet my friends, but I thought it might be awkward with..."

"With us being over?" I asked.

He nodded. "Yeah. Us."

There was nothing more I could say. Mitchell wouldn't commit even if I was staying in Toronto, but it was impossible to keep my mind from going there anyway. While I rested my head against his chest, my thoughts imagined what it would be like if we had different priorities, if we were going to be in the same city, if we hadn't grown up with the influences we'd had.

But then we wouldn't have been the same people, and I liked who we were.

"So, this is the end, huh?" I raised an eyebrow.

"Just about."

"It was fun." Fun was an understatement, but burdening him with my feelings for him wouldn't make the situation easier. It wouldn't change the fact that we had to go our separate ways.

He smiled. "Definitely." He gave me a small kiss. "Let's dance. Maybe we can convince them to play The Head and the Heart."

THE NIGHT WAS WINDING DOWN. THE MUSIC WAS SLOWING, giving Mitchell and I more time to wrap our arms around each other in the middle of the dance floor. As most of the parents and grandparents left, I no longer had to share his time with their questions and requests to cut in. When Tomas and Gillian left, I realized how late it had become.

"I should go." I sighed. "Hazel and I need to leave Nine Pines super early tomorrow morning."

There was so much to do once we got back into the city. It was time to get back to real life. I had to meet up with a group for class before my Sunday night shift at the bar. Hazel had a meeting with a client to go over some details for a case going to court on Monday.

"It was a good week. For me at least," Mitchell said. "I hope it was for you, too."

It had been better than good. I planned to tell him it has been one of the best weeks I'd had in a long time, but someone tapped on my shoulder. I turned to find Nina grinning at me.

She grabbed my wrist and pulled me close to her. Nina tipped her head to the rest of the bridesmaids who were all finishing what was left in their glasses. "So, we're heading out."

"What?" I looked between her and the two groomsmen who were bringing over the coats. "What about the take down? I said I couldn't stay to clean up. I have to head back to Toronto first thing in the morning."

"We are having an after party at the motel. Come by when you're done here," Nina said. She gave Mitchell a casual wave before turning back to her group.

If I was the only one to stay, it would take me hours to clean up. I'd never get to sleep.

I rushed across the dance floor to catch up to them.

Sliding to a stop, I put myself between them and the door. My hands shot out in front of me, stopping them from going anywhere. "Hey, I can't stay. I have a school project and I have to work. You guys knew this. You need to help with the clean-up."

"We'll come by in the morning. It's not that big of a deal," Amber said. If Nina said it, I might have believed it. But growing up with Amber, I knew how flakey she could be. As much as I loved my cousin, I knew taking her word at face value was a risk.

"We have an agreement with the venue," I said. My voice was shaking. "All the decor needs to be down tonight and they can do the rest tomorrow."

"I think it sounds like something you can handle," Amber said with a laugh. Amber's eyes shifted to Nina to take in her response.

I bit the inside of my cheek to keep from calling her out.

My brother appeared with his coat. He still looked sober, but I couldn't imagine he would stay that way after going to the after party.

"What's going on?" Mitchell asked, putting an arm around my waist.

"Do you want to come to the after party at Nina's motel room?" Amber asked.

Defeat settled onto my shoulders. I wrapped my arms around myself and glanced away.

Lucas tossed his coat onto one of the chairs. "Charlie, go home. We got this."

I looked up at my brother, surprised. He was actually putting aside the chance to party, to get high, to stick around and help. I wanted to hug him.

"Yeah," Mitchell said, giving my side a squeeze. "You've done enough for this wedding. Head home, we got this. All of us." He turned to look at the rest of the wedding party. Amber sighed.

"Actually, *we* got this." Lucas tipped his head at Amber. "Mitchell, can you make sure Charlie gets home safely?"

"Definitely." Mitchell turned me away from the group. "Let's get our coats."

"*Thank you*," I mouthed over my shoulder to my brother. Lucas gave me a subtle wink.

If tonight had to be my last night with Mitchell, I was glad we would have a quiet moment to say goodbye.

29

———————

MITCHELL

Saying goodbye came easy to me. I'd perfected the right tone and words. It was supposed to be casual and in good fun. It didn't feel like either of those things. I wanted to justify my disappointment for the end by assuming it was because I was away from my friends or because I needed that connection. But the truth was much more simple than that. I liked her.

A lot. Definitely more than I wanted to or expected to.

"Well, here we are," she said as we walked up the driveway. She squeezed my hand and stopped me when we reached the front door.

"Yeah, we are."

"I didn't think it would be awkward, because like...we knew." Charlie's laugh was abrupt. She glanced up at me with her doe eyes.

I pushed a loose strand of hair behind her ears. I'd been with many beautiful women in my time, but none I wanted to stare at as much as Charlie. Every time I looked at her, I found another feature to focus on: the freckles on her cheeks, the faint lines around her eyes when she smiled, the ring of yellow around her pupil. I would miss all those details.

"Maybe we'll see each other at The Head and the Heart show," I said.

She shook her head. "I'm not going. I used my savings to help my parents with the bills."

"Oh." That was more disappointing than I thought it would be. I thought about asking her if we could make plans, meet up when my tour was over, when things calmed down for a bit.

But I knew it wasn't the right thing to do. It would mean dragging things out. We both deserved our closure.

"You're leaving for tour on Monday. You're getting back on the road, living your dreams, right?"

"Right."

She was right. Those were my dreams. The band was everything I'd ever wanted up until that point. I wanted to be on the road. The gig life was for me. Somehow, those things hadn't seemed as important in the week I'd been home. For the past week, I'd allowed myself to get caught up in her, but that was over now. Our paths had crossed momentarily, but the lives that lay ahead of us ran parallel.

"And I'll be here." She looked at the front door of her parents' house. She turned to look at me. Her eyes looked glassy. "I know we're going our own way, but I'm not alone in feeling like this was something, right? Like, this wasn't as casual and detached as we meant for it to be?"

I didn't know what to say.

"Oh." She stepped back. "It's just me."

"No." I reached for her wrists. Even though it would make the transition complicated, I couldn't have her assuming she was alone in it. It would hurt her and I realized then I would do anything to avoid that.

"I know you are used to—"

"Charlie." I took her face in my hands and chuckled. "I agree. It wasn't just some meaningless hookup. And I can see you're doubting me, but I'm being honest."

She tilted her head like she still didn't believe me.

I kissed the tip of her nose. "I've never had trouble saying goodbye before. Not to anyone. This one isn't simple."

She stepped into me again, letting me wrap my arms around her.

"I don't know if it is easier or harder knowing that you feel the same way," she said against my chest. "But I'm still glad we did this. It was really nice getting to know you."

"It was nice getting to know you, too." I swallowed hard. "Even though moving back to Nine Pines isn't what you envisioned for your life, what you're doing for your family is really amazing. I think it takes a special person to do that."

We stayed in the hug for a full minute. I could feel her breathing against me. It was impossible to tell if I could feel her heartbeat or my own. I would miss that.

"I should go," she said in a whisper. "I have to at least try to sleep."

I stood there, unsure of what to do as she unlocked the door and stepped inside. Every instinct told me to follow her, but my friends were at my mom's house. My grandmother was expecting me in the morning. Charlie needed to sleep, because our real lives began again in the morning.

"Hey," I said. "One more thing."

I stepped through the doorway and wrapped my arms around her waist. She slipped her arms around my neck and pulled me toward her. I took in every inch of her face. Those were the eyes I would write songs about, the lips I would dream about, the touch I would long for.

She kissed me and I kissed her back.

But then I let her go, because it was the right thing to do, even if felt like I was making a massive mistake.

30

CHARLIE

I HADN'T SLEPT MORE THAN AN HOUR BECAUSE I COULDN'T STOP thinking about the decision I'd made. Saying goodbye to Mitchell hurt more than I'd expected, but that compounded with my lack of sleep and the plan to let my boss know I was quitting, and it was all too much. I pulled my knees to my chest and wrapped my arms around them.

There was a quiet knock on the door before it opened.

"Charlie, it's time to get up. Hazel is on her way to get some breakfast before you two leave."

I rolled over and looked at my mom. She was still in her robe. Her face looked fresh, free of all the previous night's make-up. I hadn't even bothered to remove my shapewear before throwing myself onto my bed.

"What's wrong, sweetheart?" She asked, stepping into my room.

"Is our youngest too hungover for bacon and eggs?" My dad sang as he stuck his head in through the doorway. His hair was sticking up all over the place. My mom reached out and attempted to smooth it out. She failed.

"I'm not hung over." I groaned.

"What's wrong?" My dad asked. He tilted his head at me, giving me a pouty look like that of a golden retriever.

"I just asked the same thing." My mom looked at him. They said something with their eyes that I couldn't decipher before turning to look at me. I almost told them I was fine, but they sat down on the edge of my bed.

My dad gave my foot a squeeze. "Spill it."

"It feels like so many things. Like, I had a good time with Mitchell and it's over. And I'm going to work tonight to tell my boss I'm done working there when the semester ends. And I'm sad about it, because I love that job," I told them. "I'm going to miss it when I move back at Christmas. And I feel like I should tell you, I don't really want to move home."

I felt sick that the words came out. I never wanted them to feel like I hated the idea of supporting them. For so long, I made sure they assumed I needed to be there, so they wouldn't refuse my help, and so they wouldn't find a way to convince me they didn't need it. My emotions got the better of me.

"We should tell her," my dad said in a whisper to my mom.

"I think she has enough on her plate right now."

"She needs to have enough time to change her plans."

I pulled myself up into a sitting position, using the covers to hide that I slept in my shapewear. "What are you guys talking about? What do you mean, change my plans?"

My father sighed.

My mother straightened her shoulders and said, "We weren't sure how to tell you this. We were hoping we would stumble on a good moment, but there doesn't seem to be one. We're not staying in Nine Pines, Charlotte. Your father got a job in Ottawa."

"You're moving? To Ottawa?"

My father puffed up his chest and grinned widely at me.

He pretended to dust his shoulder off and said, "I landed a job at the Canada Revenue Agency."

"You're going to be working for the CRA?" I blinked, unsure of what to say. I'd spent so much time planning for my return, coming to terms with giving up my life in Toronto. "How are you paying for the move? Do you need help? I thought you were going to lose the house."

My parents exchanged a look before turning back to me.

"What do you mean?" My mom asked.

"All the renovations. And I found a internet and phone bill. It was overdue and I..." I stopped, noticing the confused look on their faces.

My father patted my foot and said, "Charlotte, the renovations are to get the house ready to sell."

"And the overdue bill is Lucas'. He just needed a hand to get back on track," my mother explained. The way my parents glanced at each other again told me it wasn't a one-time situation. They had been avoiding the truth to protect Lucas.

"So, you guys aren't struggling?"

They chuckled to each other.

My mother said, "We're actually in a great place, for once. So much so that we want to help with your student loans since we don't have a place to offer you after you graduate."

I opened my mouth and closed it again. After all the years of worrying, immense relief flooded my entire body. I relaxed back against the headboard and stared at them. I couldn't believe my luck. Hazel had been right in pushing me to talk to them. If I hadn't told them the truth, I might have messed up things at work or talked Hazel into giving someone else the room before I found out.

"You're actually good? Financially?" I watched their faces for any signs of deception. There was no indication they were just saying it to please me, to reassure me. My father was grinning so widely, his eyes were crinkling. My mom's eyes softened as she stared at me.

"Charlotte, we're fine." My father got to his feet. "So, you're not quitting your job if you don't want to. But if you need a place to stay after school, it'll have to be in Ottawa and not Nine Pines."

My mother stood too. "Now, come downstairs and get some breakfast because you girls are going to be late if you don't get on the road within the next half hour."

They left the room, shutting the door behind them. Alone in my room, I climbed out of bed and danced around in my shapewear.

I didn't have to quit my job. I could stay in Toronto. I didn't have to give up my room in Hazel's apartment. I could live the life I wanted.

Then my thoughts turned to Mitchell. I sat down on the corner of my bed. A new layer of sadness blanketed my disappointment over the situation. Knowing that Mitchell and I both had our own reasons for going in separate directions made it easier. Now that I had no excuse, it was worse. I'd have to come to terms with the fact that Mitchell had different priorities and I wasn't one of them.

31

MITCHELL

Even though my grandma invited us all over for breakfast, it was Mo who took over in the kitchen. He'd gone out to pick up groceries before anyone woke up. He had a plan and no one could convince him otherwise. He even promised to make sure there were plenty of left overs for the family sleeping off the post-wedding hangover in the spare room.

My grandma showed Camila around her sunroom and even posed for a handful of pictures among the plants. Only after my second cup of coffee did I feel awake enough to sit up straight in the chair.

"Breakfast is served," Mo called as he set the massive frying pan into the centre of the table. The smell of onions and tomatoes filled the air. My stomach groaned, but it still took me a full minute to get the energy up to stand.

"This looks amazing," my grandmother said as she looked down at the breakfast casserole Mo had created. The eggs were cooked to perfection with the yolk spilling over everything in the pan. Mo had poured orange juice and coffee for everyone.

Camila let out a long "mmmm".

I waited while everyone served themselves, focusing my attention on my third cup of coffee.

"Why didn't you invite your lady friend over for breakfast as well?" My grandma asked when I finally filled my plate. Mo and Camila stared at me. I pretended not to notice. They had inquired about how things had ended, but I hadn't been in the mood to discuss it. I still wasn't.

"She said she had to go back to Toronto super early this morning," Camila told my grandma when I didn't answer.

Mo cleared his throat.

"We're going back to our lives," I said. I shrugged, not once, but twice. "No sense in dragging it out."

"That's disappointing," my grandma said. "I always liked the Whittaker family. They're good people."

I watched Mo and Camila give their breakfast plates their full attention. The move was so obvious that it frustrated me. There was no reason for it to be awkward. Charlie and I had a plan. We'd had our fun. It was over.

I put my fork and knife down on the table and said, "Tomorrow Forever July hits the road for two weeks. That's my focus. The band is life. I'm not giving that up."

"Why would you have to give it up?" Camila asked. Mo still didn't look up from his plate.

"I watched my parents give up everything for each other just for it to end in an epic disaster," I told them. "Honestly, I'm not looking to do that to myself or to someone else. We shouldn't give up everything for another person."

Mo looked me in the eye for the first time since we sat down and nodded, like he understood where I was coming from. I appreciated the back-up, because Camila's sigh felt like betrayal. I picked up my fork and grabbed some of the hash browns in front of me, shoving them into my mouth.

My grandma set her fork down and dabbed her mouth with the napkin Mo had laid out for each of us. She cleared her throat and turned in her chair so she was staring right at me. "Mitchell, you're being foolish."

"Am I?" I asked with a mouthful of food. I swallowed. "My parents resent each other for having to put their dreams on hold for each other or for me and my brother. Whatever. I learned from their mistakes."

My grandmother laughed. "No, your parents resented each other because they're selfish people who had no business being married in the first place."

Mo tapped Camila on the arm and nodded. I turned to tell them to stay, that I wasn't interested in the conversation, but Camila shook her head.

"We'll be right back. I want to get a picture of Mo and the tree in your front yard while the light is coming through the window like that."

My grandmother didn't wait until they left the table before going on. "Your parents were so destructive because they are very much alike. They are both deeply unhappy people and they use everyone and everything as an excuse for their feelings instead of realizing that they are their own enemies. My son blamed your mother for ruining his career as a musician, but he never committed to his music and he wasn't even good at it. But instead of putting in the work, instead of putting in an effort to become better, he blamed your mother."

"But my mom—"

"Your mother didn't have a stable upbringing. You know that. And instead of dealing with the trauma that faces her, she throws herself from one person to another, hoping for them to fix things." My grandmother reached across the table and squeezed my hand. "You and Tomas aren't like your parents. You have more emotional intelligence than the two of them combined, but you have blind spots."

I covered her hand with my own. "Blind spots?"

"You might not realize how emotionally intelligent you

are, but I know it. Your friends know it." She looked me in the eye and said, "Don't be like your parents. Don't look for the easy way out. Putting everything into the band and cutting everything else out, that's the easy way."

"It doesn't feel easy."

"Pushing away people you care about, it'll end up making life much harder in the future."

I thought about why I came to Nine Pines in the first place. Admitting it to myself had been hard in the beginning, but spending time with my grandmother and Charlie and even having a few moments of bonding with my brother had made me realize I'd been craving that intimacy for a while.

My friends in the city were important to me, but my connection to Nine Pines wouldn't go away no matter what I did. Charlie understood that. Tomas and my grandma understood that. They knew and understood a piece of me most people didn't. I hadn't realized how much I'd needed that until that wedding invitation arrived.

"It sounds like you've been waiting to say all of this for a while."

She winked at me. "I had the same conversation with your brother almost a year ago."

It had been almost a year ago that Tomas posted a picture across all social media platforms with the caption "she said yes." I wondered if Tomas' conversation happened before or after he proposed.

"But he gave up everything for Gillian," I told her. "All his plans, all his dreams, and he just sacrificed it for a woman."

If Tomas hadn't started dating Gillian, he would still be living on the west coast, surfing, rock climbing, doing all the things he wanted to do. Instead, he'd bought a house in Nine Pines. He was settling down, which was the opposite of everything he wanted.

"You should talk to your brother, Mitchell. I think you two can learn a lot from each other," my grandma said.

I wondered what fear brought Tomas to my grandmother for help. When a chance arose, I would ask him. I wanted to hear the fears he'd been dealing with and how he was able to push through. If anyone understood, it would be Tomas.

I patted her hand. "I will. When I get back from tour, he's coming to the city."

"It'll be good for both of you." My grandmother picked up her fork and said, "Go get your friends. Tell them to stop hanging around the front door like strangers."

I turned in my chair to see exactly what they were doing. Mo and Camila were looking for a cue to come back inside. Mo had leaned toward the window and I made eye contact with him as he peeked inside.

When I opened the front door, they both sighed with relief.

"It's colder out here than I thought," Camila said, rubbing her arms. Mo pushed past me to get into the warmth of the house.

"Come eat," Mo called as he made his way into the kitchen. "We need to hit the road in twenty minutes or we'll never make it back for a jam sesh."

"And we have to go to Chase's tonight," Camila said. "I need to get some photos edited before then."

It was the end of the week. Life was going back to the way I'd been wanting, but my whole body was heavy with hesitation. All the things I wanted before didn't seem as important. I still needed my band and I still wanted to tour, but there was so much more too.

Before shutting the door behind me, I glanced down the street at Charlie's parents' house. I knew she was gone, but I couldn't help myself.

32

CHARLIE

THE CROWD OF PEOPLE WAITING TO GET DRINKS AT THE FRONT bar was four deep, but I took a second to turn my focus on Hazel who leaned on the sticky counter. While I poured us matching shots of tequila, Hazel leaned in closer and said, "Don't give up your day off yet. Maybe we can find you some cheap The Head and the Heart tickets. We can go together, so it's not awkward if you run into — him."

I pushed one of the shot glasses toward her. We were in sync as we picked them up, clinked them together, and tipped them into our mouths. I chased mine with sparkling water from where I kept it in the ice well. Hazel chugged what was left of her beer before slamming it onto the counter.

I swallowed down the burning as I asked the next patron what I could get them. As I popped the lids off the beers they requested, I told Hazel, "I don't think so."

I took the man's money and tossed it into the register. He waved away the change, so I tossed it into the bucket beneath the counter. The music was so loud I couldn't hear as it landed on the other tips from the night. I nodded at the next person, a man with bright blue eyes and a wide smile. He was handsome.

"Come on," Hazel groaned. "Don't pick up a shift."

"Two double vodka sodas," the blue-eyed man said to me. He winked. All I could muster up was a vague smile as I grabbed cups from the stack.

"You're staying in Toronto," Hazel said. "Why don't you text him and see if he's interested in getting together?"

I grabbed the bottle of vodka from the counter behind me and began free pouring it into each of the cups. "Because he likes his single life and I can't just have another casual thing. Not with Mitchell, anyway."

Vodka-Soda Man leaned across the bar and shouted over the music. "How about with me?"

"Sorry, can you repeat that?" I asked, pretending I didn't hear. Sometimes they took the out and followed up with 'nothing'. Only the boldest tried again. It was one of the things I picked up over the few years working at The Dive. Some of the other bartenders were better at repelling those types of comments, but I could hold my own.

"I could show you a good time," he doubled down.

Hazel wrinkled her nose and said, "Dude, does this work for you?"

He turned his attention to Hazel and said, "Was I talking to you? No. So, shut it."

Instead of handing him the vodka sodas, I pushed them both toward Hazel. I leaned toward the man and said, "Get your drinks somewhere else."

He raised both middle fingers at me before turning around and leaving the bar. Immediately, a couple filled in his place. They were too occupied with each other to notice the way he shoved them as he passed.

After I took their order, I grabbed a sip from one of the vodka sodas.

"A lot has happened between you and Mitchell since you guys made those rules. You never know what's changed with him since then. When he gets back from tour, you should text him, see where his head is at."

What she said made sense. I was building my life in the city. I was making plans for what kind of future I was going to have there. Mitchell had his own life, his own plans, but I wondered if he wanted any small part in mine.

If I didn't ask, I would never know. As Mitchell told me, communication was key.

The one thing holding me back was the sliver of hope I'd managed to maintain was fragile. As much as I wanted to know for sure, there was a comfort in not knowing. I was able to trick myself into believing that he wanted me and he wanted to be with me. There would be no coming back if he told me flat out that it was only a one-time thing, merely a distraction from real life.

"Are you going to do it?" Hazel asked between sips of the vodka sodas.

"When is he back?" I asked.

She held up a finger and pulled up the tour schedule on her phone while I continued to serve other people. I was opening a tallboy of PBR when she turned her phone screen toward me.

"Last show is next Friday, so they should be home Saturday or Sunday at the latest, I'm sure." Hazel grinned at me.

"Fine," I said as I set the beer on the counter. "The Monday after they get back, I'll text him."

Hazel did a terrible job of trying to hide her smile behind her plastic cup.

33

—————

MITCHELL

Following through with Tomas' request, we went to a sports bar before we headed to the club with my friends. As soon as we got there, I could tell he was in his element. He adjusted his voice to be loud enough over the voices all around us. He barely looked at the menu before ordering. As he ate his wings, his face was in a smile as if he'd tried them for the first time.

"You can invite your friends if you're missing out on some crucial bro time," Tomas said after wiping his hands with a lemon-scented wet napkin. He sat back in his chair as the waitress came by with our second pints.

"Nah, I just spent two weeks with them. We'll meet up with them at the club," I said. Forever July had returned to the city early that morning. I'd slept all day in preparation for the arrival of my brother and Gillian. "Are you sure Gillian's good at the apartment?"

I had no problem leaving Gillian alone at my place, but I didn't want either of them to feel like she wasn't welcome there. She was my sister-in-law and I was looking forward to getting to know her better.

"She's probably watching her shows. The cabin we rented

for the honeymoon didn't have cable or Wi-Fi, so she's been desperate to binge basically everything." Tomas chuckled. Instead of some Caribbean destination or somewhere in Europe, they'd headed north to a place they rented far away from everyone.

"Yeah, now that you mention it, I have a question. You live in Nine Pines, so why would you go to another secluded town for your honeymoon?" I asked. I pitched my voice upward so he would know it wasn't a judgment. We were still getting used to talking to each other, and I didn't want him to assume my question was rude.

"We wanted to go dirt biking," Tomas said. He smirked. "We don't get to do much of that since I moved back here."

My eyebrows arched upward. "Gillian likes dirt biking?" There was no hiding my surprise now. The idea of Gillian on a dirt bike could make me laugh, but the truth was, I didn't know her well enough to make that call.

"She doesn't love it," Tomas admitted as he watched a group of guys cheering at something on the television. "But she knows I do. We make sure that we both get involved in each other's interests. Something I learned from mom and dad's mistakes."

"That sounds... healthy." I blinked. Tomas wasn't the boy I remembered. He'd changed so much since he left for British Columbia. Going out west had been good for him. Just like being away from mom and dad had been good for me. I hoped that with him back in my life, maybe I could get to the place he was at.

"It is. I used to think it was all or nothing. I let that ruin my relationship with Gillian the first time around," he told me. He sipped his beer before he went on. "It's not all or nothing though, Mitch. I know they made us believe that, but we shouldn't be taking any life lessons from either of them." Tomas smirked at his own statement.

"But how do you make it work? You get to go dirt biking

sometimes, but you don't get to live where you want to? And you have to have chickens." It didn't make sense. It didn't seem like a fair trade off.

"It's more than a fair trade off. Gillian and I work well together. We give each other the space to be ourselves. Believe it or not, it's possible to have it all. You might have to make some changes, but the core parts of you, that doesn't go anywhere," he explained.

I wondered what life would be if I didn't throw all my energy behind the band. I wondered if I would be able to sleep at night, if the loneliness wouldn't follow me from place to place. It would have been nice to have more than one thing to look forward to. The idea of coming home to someone after the tour was becoming more appealing every day.

"One," he said, holding up a finger, "I have Gillian. That's my priority. Two, when I want to go dirt biking or rock climbing, I can do that. Sure, Gill doesn't always come along, but I can do that. Three, I moved back here to be closer to you and Grandma."

"You did?"

"Yeah, dude. When we started talking about our future and what we wanted for a family, it occurred to me, I wouldn't ever be good without you and Grandma as part of that family."

I wiped the condensation from my pint while I took in those words. I glanced up at him and said, "Honestly. It didn't feel like that. You almost didn't invite me to your bachelor party."

Tomas nodded. He inhaled through his nose and nodded again. "All you ever talked about was getting out of Nine Pines. I had these big plans to reach out, but I was worried I'd spook you."

The statement made me chuckle. "Yeah, that tracks."

Tomas smiled too. "Glad we could have this talk."

"Me too." I raised my beer and he did the same. We clinked the glasses together before taking a mouthful.

"There are some girls staring at you," Tomas said as he set his empty pint back onto the table.

Without glancing over, I knew the table of women he mentioned. I'd noticed the look on their faces when we first entered the bar. They knew who I was. I couldn't be sure, but I thought one of them took a picture or a video while I took my jacket off.

"I saw them earlier," I told him. "Perks of the job."

Tomas sat back in his seat and laughed. "Why don't you go talk to them?"

"Nah. We're gonna meet up with the boys soon. Chase is already on his way to the bar," I explained. It was a half truth. The other half was that Charlie popped into my mind. If I wanted to talk to anyone, it would be her.

"You can't do both?"

If I could do both, it wouldn't be with some women I'd just met. I sat up straight.

"That triggered something, huh?" Tomas leaned forward to look into my eyes. "What are you thinking, little brother?"

"That it's been all or nothing for me." I grabbed the phone from the table and typed out a message to Chase.

Change of plans. Heading to The Dive.

34

———————

CHARLIE

I NOTICED HIM FROM ACROSS THE BAR. HE HAD BEEN AT THE Dive the weekend before. He had waved his middle fingers in my face before going off to annoy another bartender. Since it was early, he made his way toward me without the struggle of dodging other patrons. He pushed between two people waiting in line to be served. I tossed the couple in front of me their change and slipped past Johnny toward the storage room.

"I'm going into hiding," I said to my manager. With the door shut behind me, I sat on an untapped keg and took my phone out to text Hazel that Double-Vodka-Soda was back.

I hit send. I tried not to look at the message she'd sent only an hour ago, the one that went unanswered. She let me know Forever July was back home from the tour. She ran into Camila while buying records that afternoon and immediately texted me, reminding me to contact Mitchell.

Hazel had been relentless about wanting me to talk to him. He had been back in town for a single day, so I knew I could drag it out if I wanted to. Hazel would give me a week. I could use classes and work as an excuse, but it wouldn't last forever.

I opened my texts to Mitchell as I had almost six times since Hazel's text came in. A draft message was sitting there, ready for me to hit the send button. It consisted of only four words:

Can we meet up?

Every time I tried to type something more sentimental, I worried he might be with another woman when he received it. I didn't want the wrong person to see it. Even though it would crush me a little, I didn't want to ruin anything he had going on.

The storage room door opened and Ryan, one of the bar bouncers, stuck his head in. "Ex-boyfriend?"

"Nah," I laughed. "Just that guy that glared at me all night last week."

"Want me to kick him out?"

I shook my head with a laugh. "Nah. I just need a second before I deal with it."

Ryan squeezed into the small space with me and closed the door. "What happened?"

"He was being a dick, so I made him go to another bartender for drinks. He glared at me all night. I just don't want to deal with that."

Ryan turned and opened the storage room door. He turned back to me and asked, "Really? That dark-haired dude?"

"No, the blonde guy. Kinda muscular. Wearing the denim shirt."

Ryan's forehead wrinkled as his eyebrows pinched together. "Well, there's a different dude out there looking for you."

I got up from the keg and rubbed where it had pressed into my legs. I tucked my phone into my back pocket and peeked out the door.

Standing at the bar, talking to a woman who had been waiting for a drink when I darted away, was Mitchell. He was wearing a red flannel shirt over a white t-shirt. The sleeves were rolled up to his elbow, exposing his tattoos. I bit my bottom lip to keep from giggling.

"Is *that* an ex-boyfriend?" Ryan asked, following my gaze.

"We've hung out," I told him.

"Ha!" Ryan clapped me on the back. "He's hot. Go get him, dude."

From the shelf by the door, I grabbed the first bottle I could find. With whiskey in hand, I stepped back out behind the bar. Mitchell's attention redirected from the woman to me.

A jolt of electricity shot through me as our eyes connected. I'd been waiting two weeks for it, while also fearing I wouldn't have it again. The current continued through me, making my legs weak and my hands shaky.

A smile stretched across his face as I took cautious steps toward him.

"Hi," I said as I reached the bar. I set the whiskey down and grab a cup from the stack next to me. I kept my hands busy making a drink while I asked, "How have you been? How was the tour?"

I wished we were anywhere but in the loud bar. It was hard to hear him. There was a counter between us. I wanted to be so close to him I could feel his body's warmth. The soft skin of his freshly shaven face beckoned me to touch it. I wanted his hands on me.

"Do you have a break?" He asked. "Can we talk for a minute?" He was tapping his fingers on the bar as if he was nervous. It was making me more jittery.

"Probably not for another hour," I told him.

The conversation could only go one way without breaking my heart. He owed me nothing, but I wanted to believe I was as important to him as he was to me. I wasn't sure I would be able to hold back tears if he didn't tell me he'd been thinking about me the entire time we'd been apart.

"You can take your break now. I can open beers for fifteen minutes," Bouncer Ryan said. I turned to look past him to my manager, Johnny. Johnny nodded and gave me a small wink. I handed the drink to Mitchell before wiping my hand on the bar towel shoved in my back pocket. I ducked under the counter and walked around until we were face to face.

It had only been two weeks, but the days stretched on for what seemed like forever. Even though we'd ended things, I was waiting for the day he would be back in the city. I wondered if I was alone in feeling that.

He took a sip of his drink and said, "You make the best Manhattans."

I took his arm and led him away from the bar toward the back exit. If I was going to take my break, I wanted to do so where I could hear him. I didn't want to miss a single word.

"I'm glad you're here. I've been meaning to text you," I said.

"And I've been meaning to text you." He smiled. "I want to ask you what you're doing next Friday."

Next Friday would have been The Head and the Heart show. I pushed open the door to the alley. A blast of cold air pushed its way in as we made our way out. I wrapped my arms around myself as we faced each other, huddling against the building.

"Hazel and I were going to sit around our apartment eating junk food and watching High Fidelity." I laughed and shrugged.

"Do you think you could postpone? I was wondering if you wanted to come with me to The Head and the Heart." His dark eyes were smiling just as much as his lips.

"You got tickets for The Head and the Heart?"

"Camila is getting you and I backstage." He puffed out his chest slightly.

I didn't hesitate. I threw my arms around his neck, pulling

him close into a hug. The time we spent apart felt non-existent. "Yes, I'll go."

He squeezed me so tight. His body was almost hot against mine. I didn't want him to let go. I didn't want space between us. Hugs with Mitchell made me realize how I'd never been as comfortable with anyone the way I was with him. When our bodies were flush together, I didn't think about how long was too long for a hug or if he thought I smelled good. With Mitchell, I focused on how nice it was to be together, holding each other.

When we inevitably slipped out of the hug, the cold air made me shiver.

"I decided I wanted to see you as much as I can before you move back to Nine Pines," he told me. "I would like to call it a date, if you're okay with that."

"A hundred percent okay with that," I said. I was about to tell him I had no plans to move back to Nine Pines, but I could see he wasn't finished speaking.

He sucked in a deep breath and said, "And, when you're in Nine Pines, I was hoping I could still come see you. Maybe you could come here too sometimes."

The frigid air was forgotten. I stared up at him, trying not to giggle, trying not to blurt words out at him. By the way his weight shifted from foot to foot and how his fingers were tapping on the plastic cup, I realized he was working through some thoughts. He needed a minute to process. I bit my cheek to keep from speaking.

"I've been thinking about the way we ended things. We had a nice goodbye, but I'm not sure if I'm ready to give you up, Charlie. You're selfless. You're motivated. You're beautiful. And, honestly, you're one of the select few who I don't feel restless around. When I'm with you, I'm content."

I pressed my lips together, holding back my smile while he went on.

"I wanna ask, would you be interested in giving things

between us a solid try? Like, dating and monogamy and all that stuff?"

"What about the band?" I asked him.

"I don't think I have to choose, do I?" He asked.

I shook my head. "Definitely not. I would never want you to."

"And I know your family is your priority and I will never get in the way of that. I want to be there to support you and help with whatever comes up, if I can."

I reached out and took his wrist, letting him know it was my turn to talk. "My parents are moving to Ottawa."

"What?" His eyes darted around my face as if searching for answers. "What does that mean? Do you have to move with them?"

"My dad got a job with the CRA. A good paying job." I beamed. "And that means, I'm staying in Toronto."

He laughed. "What? They're leaving Nine Pines and you're staying here?"

"Yeah, they're leaving in January and I'm staying in the city. When I finish classes, I'm going to work here full time, maybe try to get a management position here eventually. Or somewhere else. Whatever happens."

Even though I trusted Mitchell to be honest, a small part of me knew there was a possibility the information might change things. Mitchell had a lifestyle that he loved. I never wanted to stand in the way of him living all the ways he dreamed of.

He tipped his head back a little and looked me over. Then, cautiously, he asked, "This is a good thing, right?"

"I think it is. Do you?" I arched a single eyebrow.

With his free hand, he tugged at the hem of my shirt. "One hundred percent."

I giggled. "Okay, good."

His face split into a wide smile. "I'm gonna kiss you now, alright?"

I didn't wait for him to lean in. I pushed up on my toes, bumping our noses together.

"I like you, Charlie Whittaker," he whispered against my mouth.

"Oh, you like me?" I teased. I allowed my lips to brush against his. After a brief kiss, I pulled back and said, "I like you too. And I have to admit, it's been kinda weird not talking to you every day."

He pressed his forehead against mine for a second while he said, "I'm glad you feel the same."

I reached up and brushed some hair from his face before pushing my lips against his.

I couldn't believe how only three weeks ago I'd been ready to give up everything I worked for, everything I'd become, only to be standing there with so much future ahead of me. I would be able to move forward with all the things I wanted in my life, with the people I wanted in my life.

"I'm freezing," I said, pressing my cheek into his. "Can we go inside?"

"Only if you promise to keep these Manhattans coming for the rest of the night."

"With one stipulation. If I keep making you drinks, you walk me home tonight." I grinned up at him.

Mitchell rubbed my arms, trying to keep them warm. "I'm clearly coming out on top in this deal."

I kissed him. "Nah, we both are."

35

———

MITCHELL

Before Chase brought the van to a stop, I was unlocking my seat belt and grabbing my bag from where I'd stashed it by my feet. The rest of the boys were still asleep in the back, so I pushed the door open as silently as possible.

"The first time away is always the hardest," Chase reminded me for the tenth time since we hit the road over a week ago. "You're never going to get used to this, but it's easier."

"Thanks, man." I gave his shoulder a squeeze before climbing out of the van. After a promise to get together for some food and beers later in the week, I closed the van door and eased my way across the icy sidewalks. I yanked open the heavy, metal door leading to my apartment and sprinted up the stairs.

My legs were weak from sitting in the car since we crossed at the border. The three-and-a-half-hour drive once back in Canada usually went too fast. The end of the tour meant being alone in my apartment. It meant no one to talk to when I wanted to stay in bed. It meant no one to talk to when the quiet became too much.

But, this time, I couldn't wait to get home.

I unlocked the door to my apartment and eased it open. I set my bag against the wall and slipped out of my shoes without turning on a single light. There was enough of an orange glow coming in through the windows.

Even from where I stood, the outline of her body was visible in the soft light from the street. Her back was to me as if waiting for me to crawl behind her, tuck myself against her shape.

It didn't matter how many times I returned home or woke to find her still in my bed; it always made me smile to find her beneath my sheets. I undressed as silently as possible, leaving my clothes in a pile on the concrete floor. I pulled back the covers and slipped beneath them.

I didn't touch her. Not right away. My fingers and toes were still too cold. I rubbed my hands together, hoping they would warm faster so I could place them on her skin. It had been too long since I'd had her body against mine.

Before even a shred of warmth penetrated my fingers, Charlie rolled over toward me. Her hair was stuck to her face. Her eyelids were hardly open. She said nothing and buried her face into my neck. She smelled like peppermint shampoo. I closed my eyes as I breathed her in.

"I missed you," I said into her hair.

She planted a kiss on my collarbone before nuzzling closer to me.

Even if I didn't know it at the time, I'd been spending years needing what Charlie and I had. For the first few weeks we were together, I cursed myself for not being open to such a relationship. Things were so good between us I couldn't understand why I had been avoiding the commitment for so long.

Being away from her made me realize how much had gone on in my life since autumn. I'd made peace with the fact my parents would never be who I wanted them to be. I was getting to know my brother better and spending more time with my grandmother. All those things had changed me, prepared me. If Charlie and I had met under different circumstances, it would have been a wasted opportunity. I wouldn't have been ready for her.

"Charlie," I whispered.

"Yeah?"

"I'm not lonely when I'm with you."

Even in her half sleep, the corners of her mouth turned up. She nuzzled into me and whispered, "Good."

"Even when I'm on the road."

She made a little rumbling sound to let me know she was listening, but sleep was pulling her back. I kissed the top of her head. I could tell her tomorrow, when she was awake and when I was feeling rested.

"I love you," I whispered into her hair.

She tipped her head back on the pillow and blinked at me. The seconds ticked past. I worried it was the wrong time, that our time apart made her change her mind. I'd been so certain that she would feel the same, but once I'd said it I wasn't so sure.

The words were out there. I wouldn't and didn't want to take them back.

"You okay?" I asked her when she was quiet for too long. "You don't have to say it back if you're not ready. While we were apart, I had time to process the magnitude of my feelings. I don't want to rush you just because I had that time to—"

She pressed a finger to my lips. I kissed it.

"I'm just trying to wake up," she whispered.

I smiled. "You don't have to."

She propped herself up on one arm and blinked a few times to clear her eyes. "I just wanted to be awake to tell you I love you, too."

ACKNOWLEDGMENTS

Of all the plots I have sitting in documents and notebooks, Ready to Fall wasn't one of them. It never even occurred to me to write from Mitchell's perspective. Until now!

When After the Party was released, more than a handful of people told me they needed more from the characters they met in my debut novel. It was that feedback from people who read and enjoyed After the Party that encouraged me to write this story.

I will be forever grateful to everyone who asked for more from me.

After the Party was written for me, because I couldn't get it out of my head. Ready to Fall was written for you.

I hope you enjoyed reading it as much as I enjoyed writing it.

ABOUT THE AUTHOR

A.K. Ritchie hails from a small city in Southwestern Ontario. She loves writing contemporary fiction with a focus on Romance and Coming-of-Age stories. The music she loves, the people she's met, and the places she's been influences most of what she writes.

When not writing in coffee shops or curled up in her bed scrolling through social media, A.K. Ritchie enjoys seeing live music, spending time in nature, going on road trips, and meeting new people.

A.K. Ritchie is the author of <u>After the Party</u> and <u>Ready to Fall</u>.

 facebook.com / AuthorRitchie

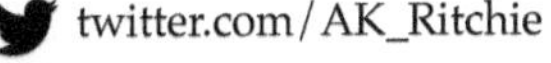 twitter.com / AK_Ritchie

instagram.com / a.k.ritchie

ALSO BY A.K. RITCHIE

After the Party